Head Rush (Head Case Trilogy Book One)

by

Jason Blacker

PUBLISHED BY:
Lemon Tree Publishing
Copyright © 2013
Jason Blacker

Visit www.JasonBlacker.com on the web to stay up to date

Editing: Laurel Berkel

ISBN: 9781927623367

For my angel, my wife and my son, my sun

Table of Contents

3:33 AM

Westmount, Montreal

Amaury Querry is in bed. He's been sleeping for almost four hours now. His eyes flutter as he enters deep REM sleep. The sleep of dreams. This is the first time he will enter into his dream state tonight, and it is also the very last time he well will enter dream state. Ever again.

Next to Amaury is his wife, Louise. If you crept into this dark room, in this huge mansion of a house, and stared at them side by side as they slept with the watery light of the moon spilling on them, you would not consider them man and wife.

Louise is thirty years younger than Amaury's sixty-three, almost to the day. And unlike him, she is in very good shape. He's let himself go, as a man of his stature is wont to do.

By stature, I do not mean his physical attributes but rather his material. Amaury Querry is one of the top ten richest men in Canada, but you'll not find him on any list. He's discreet. His business requires it and his customers appreciate it.

They say that there are two reasons why a young, beautiful, model-looking woman will marry a man old enough to be her father. The first is because he is physically well endowed, and the second is because he is materially well endowed.

Amaury Querry is of the latter. He is well connected around the world, for he deals in arms. And a man of his sort does not concern himself with the trifles of conscience. Not when he's just about to ink a deal worth one billion dollars—US dollars, mind you, which once upon a time used to mean something—with Iran. This morning when he wakes up—so he thinks—he'll be selling weapons of mass destruction and the means of making weapons of mass destruction to America's current devil incarnate du jour.

Amaury Querry has already had one heart attack. That was a few years ago. But being a successful businessman, he hasn't felt it necessary to heed his doctor's advice. He still has over forty pounds to lose just to make himself look presentable and to give his ticker a fighting chance.

But he loves good food and good wine. In fact, Amaury is known for his appetite for all the pleasures of the flesh. Just this evening a few hours ago, he lay down with his wife as a man does with his wife. And Louise pretended to enjoy it, as she has for some years now. But little does she know that she will no longer need to pretend. For tonight was the last time that Amaury would lie with her as husband and wife. Tomorrow, Louise will wake up and become the richest woman in Canada—until Amaury's son and daughter decide to contest. But that is a different story and not one we are interested in.

Tonight, Amaury Querry will die of a heart attack. It is a certainty because it has been planned this way. He will be murdered. And very few people will know. Only those who do the murdering.

The police will come by tomorrow and find nothing suspicious. There will be no breaking and entering. Louise will swear that it was just the two of them at home the whole night. And this is the truth. An autopsy will be performed because he is an important man in Canadian, nay, international business, and the coroner will confirm a myocardial infarction because the technique used to murder Amaury is top secret and the tools required to determine cause of death by this technique are not available in any coroner's office.

Let us watch as Amaury is murdered in his dreams. Amaury's dream has just started at 3:33 AM. In his dream he is meeting with top-level Iranian government officials. His dream, naturally, is about his meeting in the morning. The one we spoke about where he will ink a deal worth one billion dollars for his company, BattleBuilt.

Amaury has invited the three Iranians into his office. His secretary comes around and offers refreshments to everyone. The Iranians take espresso, all three of them. Amaury has the same as them. Along with Amaury, his two lawyers are present to ensure that the deal goes smoothly and everything is signed correctly.

His two lawyers are both female and both as young as his wife, Louise. They too are as attractive as her. Their skirts are short and hug their bums like second skins. These women have had breast augmentation, thanks to Amaury and BattleBuilt. Their breasts are straining to free themselves from the clutches of the annoying blouses.

The Iranians are having a hard time focusing on the documents at hand. Their eyes flit from tit to tit and back to the documents. Amaury beams like a proud father, as the Iranians admire his lawyers' assets.

This is his dream, yes, but this is how his lawyers really look.

"I trust everything is to your satisfaction?" asks Amaury, already knowing the answer. His English is perfect. You would have to listen closely in order to pick up any hint of the French, which is his mother tongue.

The senior Iranian official takes his eyes from the bursting breasts and glances at the document. He flips through it as if studying it carefully. In fact, he received a copy of this contract weeks earlier. This meeting is just a formality. The Iranian nods.

"Yes, this looks fine," he says in a thick Iranian accent.

"Then let us sign it," says Amaury.

The lawyer closest to him hands him a pen from her portfolio. He smiles at her, thinking about her naked, pink flesh, for he has known that flesh intimately.

The lawyer closest to the Iranian hands him a pen, her hand lingering a touch on his. Her bottom lip bit by her upper teeth. The Iranian swallows hard and thinks of his wife back home.

They sign the document and then exchange documents and sign each other's. All told, six copies are signed, three for each party to the contract.

"Gentleman," says Amaury, standing up and coming over to the men, "it has been a pleasure doing business with you."

The three Iranians shake hands with Amaury. He turns and is about to lead them out of the office when the lawyer—her name is Michelle—takes another pen from her pocket and clicks the top of it. Amaury notices the end is a sharp, pointed, hollow, thick gauge needle.

Before he realizes what is happening, Michelle thrusts the pen into his breast pocket, and it burrows between the ribs and stabs right into his heart. She pulls it out just as quickly.

Amaury grabs at his chest where blood is already leaking through the hole and staining his blue shirt. He looks at her with questions in his eyes; his mouth opens into an "o" as if he wished to speak. But no words come out. Amaury drops to his knees, still looking at his lawyer Michelle.

"Courtesy of Hattori Hanzo," she says, but her voice is that of a man's.

In the mansion in Montreal, Amaury Querry twitches and then lies dead. His heart has stopped. He breathes no more.

3:30 AM

Brooklyn, New York

Tomo Daisen lies comfortably on the bed. He is as comfortable as you can be with electrodes stuck on your head. Tomo, or Tom as most of his friends call him, is trying to meditate and get to those all-important Theta levels of brainwave activity.

He doesn't have long, but he doesn't need long either. He's done this before. In fact, if he thinks about it, this one will be thirty-seven. He doesn't know his victims' names and he doesn't want to know. This is about serving God and country. He trusts the people he works for. They're doing God's work. Or at the very least keeping the country safe from terrorists and others who have no respect for civilized society.

Anthony Buckles watches Tom relax from a separate room. He can see him from behind a one-way mirror. The machine Tom is hooked up to is as large as a refrigerator, but newer, smaller, and more efficient models are coming down the pipe soon.

Standing next to Anthony Buckles is Dr. Margaret Rakes. She's here to ensure that everything runs smoothly as it should. Both for Tom and for his victim. She'll get verification of the kill from the nanobot that's been planted deep inside Amaury Querry's brain.

James Seaton watches Tom enter the meditation as they had practiced hundreds of times before his first kill. He's got his thumb and forefinger on his chin, resting his elbow on the palm of his left hand.

James Seaton is a trainer, though he prefers to think of himself as a mentor. He was the first NINJA (Nano Implanted Neurally Jammed Assassin) of what had become NANA (National Agency of Nano Agents). James had wanted something more honest in their naming, something along the lines of Nano Assassins or Neural Assassins, but he was outvoted.

At least they kept the cute acronyms. Nobody, except those within NANA and the president, know about NANA, and everyone who knows about NANA except the president has nanobots implanted. This ensures that everyone involved is on the same team and silence is guaranteed. Your life depends upon it.

Finding NINJAs is not an easy task. You need the best trained military personnel with the most stable psychiatric profile almost bordering on sociopathic, and you need a commitment from them for life. Oh, and the nanobot thing, most don't like that part. But most recruits weren't volunteers so much as they were volun-told, and most get used to it.

Those who don't get used to it die in combat, serving their country. Heroes. James Seaton grins. Tom is different. He had jumped at the opportunity to join NANA He is a curious sort.

"Everything looking good, Doctor?" asks Anthony, keeping his eyes on Tom in the other room.

Maggie sits behind a computer with a full view of the meditation chamber, the room that Tom is in. The computer is hooked up to his vitals and his blood pressure. Heartbeat, respiration, and brain activity are all being monitored and shown on the screen.

Most agents need neural aids, chemicals, and drugs that help them get into the right frame of mind. Not Tom. He is Maggie's first self-reliant agent. He can enter Theta almost at will, and it is in Theta where the magic happens.

"He's just reached Theta, sir," says Maggie with a smile.

Inside the meditation room, Tom's eyes start to flitter. Maggie imagined that it was due to Tom's upbringing as a Buddhist that allows him to reach these deep states of meditation so easily. But she is curious as to why a Buddhist would end up as an assassin. He might as well be a priest.

Tom comes to life in a boardroom. He looks down at himself and notices his buxom bosoms straining to pop out from under their blouse. It always takes him a split second to gather his bearings. It is like lucid dreaming, and he does a lot of that in his spare time.

"I trust everything is to your satisfaction," said Amaury.

Tom looks over at him. Amaury is seated to Tom's right. Sometimes he doesn't get this lucky. But today is his lucky day. For his last assassination, he had to find his mark by searching through several levels of the building he was in. But today, his target is sitting next to him, and Tom is a woman. He couldn't have asked for an easier setup.

Tom notices the slow pulsating red beacon that starts as a small dot in the middle of Amaury's head and swells to the size of his head before subsiding and repeating again. Tom stops himself from smiling as he watches the big red head talk. Dreams are funny things, and he always gets a kick out of being part of his targets' dreams.

"Yes, this looks fine," says the Iranian who is staring at Tom's boobs.

Tom looks at him and wonders why he couldn't be a target instead. It's the Iranians that he really needs to wipe out. Then he understands. You've still got to deliver the nanobot, and that isn't always as easy as it sounds.

"Then let us sign it," said Amaury.

Tom hands Amaury a pen, and the woman next to him, who looks like his twin, hands the Iranian a pen and her touch lingers with his.

Tom watches Amaury sign the papers with the pen he had been given and then they sign each other's papers, and the woman to his left hands the Iranians three copies and she keeps three for herself. Tom looks at the pen that is now resting on the desk. He picks it up. This is the hardest part of any assassination.

Tom has to manipulate the target's dream without the target waking up, realizing that something went wrong in their dream.

For example, Tom is going to have to turn this pen into a heavy gauge needle and stab Amaury through the heart before he realizes what has happened. The killing has to be quick and sure. If it isn't, there is a chance of the target waking up and if that happens you've lost your chance and have to try again. Tom has never missed on his first try.

Tom has been momentarily lost in thought. The female lawyer sitting next to him has stood up. Tom sees Amaury has walked over to the Iranians and is shaking their hands. He's already got his arm around the one man's shoulders, ready to escort them out.

Tom stands up. He feels strange being in high heels and a tight dress that wraps around his thighs and makes taking large steps awkward. Yet because this is not really his body, his movements seem fluid and natural.

Tom walks up to Amaury and clicks the top of the pen. A heavy gauge needle several inches long sticks out from the end, and with a quick and practiced thrust, Tom injects it into Amaury's chest and through to his heart.

He pulls it out quickly. He only has seconds now before he loses the connection. Already the Iranians are disappearing and the lawyer who was standing next to them. Amaury is losing focus and his dream is disappearing as he dies in real life. Because Tom's and Amaury's nanobots are synced, this act of dreamy violence will cause Amaury's to fire a signal to the neuron they're attached to, which will cause his heart to stop beating.

Amaury is clutching his chest as red blood, like an ink stain, seeps through and stains his blue shirt. Amaury's mouth is open in an "o." This is where it ends.

"Courtesy of Hattori Hanzo," says Tom.

Maggie looks at the computer screen in front of her.

"We have EOL verification, sir," she says.

James Seaton smiles. He loves the cute the acronyms they came up with. Rather than saying the kill had been verified, they use EOL, end of life.

Anthony, who was standing next to him, turns around and walks up to Maggie and looks over her shoulder at the computer screen. He nods.

"Poor woman. She'll wake up to her dead husband in just a few hours," he says.

Maggie doesn't say anything. She doesn't like to think about that part of the job. The Canadians hadn't been notified of this job. In fact, now that she thinks about it, nobody is ever notified about any of their jobs. They run an autonomous ship at NANA, and that's how they like it.

In the other room, Tomo Daisen has opened his eyes. He slowly sits up and takes off the electrodes that have been placed all over his body. He's wearing only boxer briefs, and his smooth skin is cool to the touch. He has no fat; his five-foot-seven-inch frame is sinewy muscle tied taut to bone and ligaments.

Tom turns toward the one-way mirror and dangles his feet off the edge of the bed. He grins at them through the mirror.

"EOL complete?" he asks.

Maggie's voice comes through the intercom and confirms what he already knows.

On the other side of the mirror, Maggie watches Tom as he jumps off the bed and walks toward the table where he starts to put on his clothes. She feels butterflies in her stomach. He is an incredibly good-looking Japanese-American man. His black hair is thick and she imagines running her fingers through it. He is in his late thirties but he could easily pass for late twenties.

"Maggie?" Anthony is gently shaking her shoulder. She looks up at him.

"Uh, yes sir," she says, embarrassed now.

"Wrap up here. I'm going in to debrief Tom."

24

"Yes sir."

Maggie watches Anthony and James leave the cockpit, as they call it, and enter the meditation room where Tom has just finished getting dressed.

2:30 PM

Oval Office, The White House

Claude Martin is seated in the waiting room. He is wearing a gray suit that fits a bit loosely on his gangly frame. On his nose and wrapped around his ears is a pair of glasses. They too are too big for his face. Claude is a government wonk. He gives an image to that term. Upon his lap is a briefcase that he's had since his political science days at Harvard. His thin, long hands like dry twigs are resting on this briefcase. There are no rings on his fingers.

Claude is married to the job. He invented NANA, and each time there is a POTUS change, he has to come in here and flirt and cajole the new president about how important his work is.

His greatest coup is hanging onto his measly budget—measly when compared to the CIA's $13 billion—including their black budget that only the president knows about. Sure, NANA is much smaller. Claude only has 311 people under his command. The CIA has over 20,000. But that is only because he has to keep fighting all the time just to maintain the status quo.

But he is hoping that will change. The new man at the top seems reasonable. He understands the current threats and the problems that America and her allies are facing. Still, Claude's fingers tap the top of his briefcase nervously. He won't know for sure how the president feels until after today's meeting.

It was seven years ago, almost to the day, that Claude gave birth to NANA. His colleagues in the FBI, CIA and NSA thought he was crazy, but he's shown them. The work NANA does has greater effect than all three of those groups combined.

NANA is the epitome of covert ops. Claude smiles, thinking back to the days when he and Yolanda were pretty much all of NANA. President Larrison was unlike any president before or after. He was a visionary. Claude misses him. Things had never been so good for NANA during his brief three-year tenure.

He had been assassinated. The fifth president to be killed in office. The CIA covered it up, the damn cowards. They said it was a lunatic from the Mid-West, one of those militia types. But it wasn't. Claude found out the truth and it cost him his up until then cozy relationship with the CIA.

It was the Chinese. They didn't appreciate President Larrison's hardline approach to trade and Tibet. They took one of his, so Claude took three of their top men. You don't fuck with Claude Martin, not like that. He is a true patriot. He knows what is best for America and, in turn, the world.

"Why is he keeping us so long?" asks Yolanda Butts in a whispered voice.

Claude glances down at his Waltham wristwatch. It was made in 1957. It had been his father's. The last of the great American-made watches. Claude longs to bring back American industry. Bring America back to its premier place as the greatest industrial manufacturing as well as technological country on the planet. This watch reminds him of the finesse of American industrialism during her heyday. That time will come again if he has his say.

It is 2:39 PM. He frowns at his watch. Claude is punctual, almost to a fault. Nobody in his group is allowed to be more than three minutes late. The only person whose tardiness he will tolerate is the president's. He still doesn't like it though.

He looks over at Yolanda. She is his opposite in more ways than one.

To his shabby dress, she is chic. To his gangly, awkward thinness, she is athletic and ample. To his nerdy looks, she is an icon of beauty, and to his pale, white skin, she has the warmth of burnt sienna. She is his protégé and his unrequited love. They share a burning passion for seeing America retake its rightful place as the greatest nation on earth. And they share a manic fervor and dogged determination in reaching that goal.

"I sure hope this is a good sign. But I just can't seem to think it might not be," she says.

Yolanda is in a navy blue dress suit with a white blouse and matching blue neck kerchief. She has on black pumps. She looks more like a flight attendant than the second-in-command of a government agency. Still, she carries it well. Anything looks good on her, though Claude likes to imagine her naked more often than dressed.

Isn't going to happen in his lifetime. She likes him, more like an older brother. She respects him and admires his drive and dedication, but she does not find him attractive in any way.

"I've heard good things about President Towles," he says, smiling at her, trying to reassure.

His smile is becoming. It melts his stoic face into one of warmth. He is easy to like when he smiles. But it is the smile of a wolf in sheep's clothing.

Yolanda nods. She has heard the same. But this waiting is not a good sign. It has never been a good sign in her short career. A career that started just after she got out of UCLA. It took her five years to finish her undergrad while working three part-time jobs.

She figured that Claude had given her a chance. She wasn't the best student and, unlike most of the others vying for an entry-level position at Langley, she didn't have an expensive Ivy League education or come from a well-connected background. He must have seen something in her, though, and she hasn't let him down. Her drive and dedication match his, and her loyalty is unrelenting.

Over seven years they have worked together, moving up the lowly ranks until he managed to head one of the small covert ops sections covering Micronesia and area. Nothing was happening there, but Claude thought it was a good start. Until someone had it out for him and they were shut out from any further political maneuverings and climbing.

She admired how he had circumvented what was the political and career death blow that had been dealt. Somehow, from that small, dark, dead end corner in the bowels of the   he managed to resurrect a phoenix. The phoenix that now had become NANA.

Claude never told her who it was that had tried to stifle their career aspirations at the CIA, and she was the only one he brought across from there to join him in the founding of NANA.

Claude chose the cute acronyms on purpose. His former colleagues laughed at them. They didn't take him and his cute little acronym of an organization seriously. And that was his hope and goal. They belittled his organization and paid it no attention until it became too powerful to destroy, slowly earning the upper hand.

The door to the Oval Office's secretary opens up and she walks out. She is an older woman, close to retirement age. She served the last five presidents. She is good at it and political agnostic.

"The President will see you now," she says.

Claude stands up with Yolanda and allows her to enter first. He looks at his watch. It is 2:47 PM. The President had better make up for this tardiness.

11:36 PM

Over the North Atlantic

There are only the three of them in the plane. It is a private flight heading to Lisbon. It is so private that nobody actually knows this flight is happening. The FAA has been informed to ignore it and as such, flight control will make no mention of it.

They took off from a small hidden runway not far from Germantown, Maryland. Don't bother looking for it. It's well hidden and you won't find it on any of the mapping software either.

Tom is sitting across from James Seaton and next to him is Maggie Rakes. They are heading to Lisbon because that's where they will find the three Iranians who met with Amaury Querry earlier. Claude Martin is a stickler for tidying up loose ends.

It is all well and good to chop off a branch from the rotten tree but far better to actually uproot it. In Lisbon they will meet with Agent Maurice Hamilton, who is one of their best snipers. He will ensure delivery of the nanobots into these Iranians.

Tom met Maurice before. He likes him, but Maurice is not an inside man. He much prefers hands-off work like sniping, and he is damn good at it.

The thing with oneiricide, the murdering within dreams, is that the closer you are to the target, the easier it is and the more likely you are to get a swift EOL confirmation.

Theoretically, you can commit oneiricide at any distance away from your target, but NANA's rules of engagement prefer that the agent is within three hundred miles of the target. Tom's kill of Amaury was a little outside that parameter, but it went off without a hitch nonetheless.

The problem with being farther away is that there is a fraction of a delay between when you kill your target in their dreams and when the nanobot can execute the kill signal to the heart. If your target wakes up during that split second delay, their own brain signals firing will negate the nanobots ability to fire.

So, they are heading to Lisbon. Their intel suggested that the Iranians will be there for three days before heading back to Tehran. Eradicating these three men will be a detrimental blow to the Iranians.

Gen. Farzan Najafi and Gen. Armin Bukhari are two of the top military leaders in Iran and, combined, they control over half of the Iranian army. Dr. Milad Saatchi is one of only three men in Iran who has the expertise required to help Iran develop her own nuclear weapons. Deleting these three men from the Iranian political spectrum will set Iran back at least ten years, maybe more.

Tom looks out the window. It is a dark night. The stars are hard to see from the light inside the cabin. They are well over the North Atlantic, but he can't tell which side is ocean and which is sky. They could be flying upside down for all he can tell. There is no moon. It is a black night. The same pitch blackness that he experiences before connecting with the dreams of his victims.

"I can't exaggerate the importance of this next mission," says James.

Tom looks back at him. On the table are three folders that have not been opened yet. Tom nods.

"Amaury Querry was a great start, a necessary start," continues James, "but eliminating these next three men will really go far toward keeping the world much safer. So long as Iran has a gypsy's chance of getting nuclear weapons, then the world is not safe from Armageddon."

Tom thinks he sounds much like Claude. Overzealous and prone to exaggerated leaps of logic. He is fully aware of the threat that Iranian nuclear weapons pose, but to suggest that it will lead to Armageddon seems like a stretch. Not that he isn't looking forward to alleviating the risk—he is—he just doesn't seem to think the world is on the brink of nuclear war.

James opens up the top folder. "This is Dr. Milad Saatchi," he says.

A large, letter-sized black and white photo shows a very clear three-quarter profile photo of the man. He is dressed in a suit. He is clean shaven and looks young. Maybe in his early forties. He is handsome too.

"Doesn't look anything like the three men I saw in Amaury's dream," says Tom.

"I'm not surprised," says James, looking up at Tom.

"Where was the photo taken?" asks Tom.

"It was taken in Montreal just a few days ago. The day before you finished Amaury. Dr. Saatchi was educated in Oxford where he earned his Ph.D. in nuclear physics. Don't ask me what those Brits were thinking when they allowed him in to learn how to build nuclear weapons."

"In fairness," says Maggie, "this was before Iran was seen as such a threat, and he also entered under false pretenses. He came in as a refugee. A, what seemed to be, legitimate refugee."

James ignores her. "He's one of just three or four men who have the ability to build nuclear weapons. Getting rid of him is a good start."

Tom looks at him. James hands him a sheet of paper with bulleted points of information on it. Dr. Saatchi, it seems, has a weakness for young white women. He also likes to smack them around a bit.

This sort of information is helpful. It allows Tom to capture a psychological portrait of his target, which, when entering their dreams, will allow him to quickly and accurately assess the situation and meld right in.

The biggest danger in his type of work is entering the dream. It has to be done smoothly and discreetly. If you enter into someone's subconscious, which is what it is, there is a chance that the ripple of that event can wake them and you'll be hooped. Knowing as much about your target as possible allows you to slip right in past the subconscious doorman to your victims' dreams and play your role as accurately as possible until KT, or kill time.

"This is Gen. Farzan Najafi. He is a hardliner within the Iranian army and both greatly feared and respected by his soldiers," says James.

James opens up the second folder and a picture of an older man, probably in his mid to late sixties, was on top. He is next to Dr. Saatchi. It is almost a full-frontal of him. He too is dressed in a dark suit. He has a small paunch and the left side of his face is pockmarked, as if someone took a belt grinder to it and then lathered butter over.

"He suffered severe injuries during the Iran-Iraq war, as you can see in the photo," says James. "He has a hard-on for eliminating the evil, as he calls it, empire of the US, and he also has a huge hatred for Israel."

James pushes the photo aside and turns another information bulletin toward Tom. Tom looks at it. Gen. Najafi's weaknesses are pain medication, which he is addicted to, as well as liquor, which he secretly uses to help make the pain medication more effective. He is an extremely loyal and devout Shia Muslim despite abusing alcohol.

"This guy," says James, opening up the last folder, "is perhaps the most dangerous of these three men. We have nothing on him. He is a pillar of Muslim modesty, courage, and ethics. He is also the youngest general to serve in the Iranian army. He is just fifty. This is Gen. Armin Bukhari."

The photo of Gen. Bukhari shows a tall man, taller by at least half a foot than the other two. He too is dressed in a dark suit. He is a slim, average-looking man with a full but well-trimmed beard.

"He too is a devout Shia and outspoken supporter of the current Supreme Leader, and the Supreme Leader is a vocal supporter of anyone who is working actively to undermine the US and our way of life."

James pushes a type-written sheet toward Tom of a psychological overview of Gen. Bukhari. He has been married for twenty-seven years to the same woman. He has four children. Two boys and two girls. He has many commendations and he too has served with valor and diligence in the Iran-Iraq war. His pastimes include chess, running, and worship.

"Any questions?" asks James.

Tom looks at him and then at Maggie. Tom shakes his head. "No, seems fairly straightforward," he says.

"It is, but it's crucial we get it right. We have a small window of opportunity here. We have one chance to eliminate the threat. Knowing the Iranians, after they've been hit by our sniper they'll likely disappear the very next day. We can't count on them staying the three days like they're supposed to once they've been dosed."

James is leaning in toward him. Thirty-seven kills without a hitch. Tom isn't sweating it. Doing three during one evening is rare, but it is like shooting fish in a barrel. You just focus on one at a time.

4:37 PM

Lisbon, Portugal

Tom is sitting awkwardly next to Maurice Hamilton, high up on a bridge looking north towards Lisbon. The view of the Alcantara Docks is outstanding from here. But it isn't a view that's available to the public. They got up here, here being the twenty-fifth of April Bridge, masquerading as bridge inspectors. It was well worth the climb.

All the fat tourists visiting the trendy bars and shops, only created for them to unload their money, look like little upright ants. Tom brings his binoculars to his eyes and they miraculously appear as if they're now right in front of him. It gives the impression that he could just reach out and touch them.

Tom looks at his watch. Unlike Claude Martin, he wears a non-American-made chronograph. His Luminox is Swiss-made. Claude's okay with that, even though the Swiss are cowards and take no sides; they make good watches and they're close enough to be called allies.

Tom's Luminox reads 4:38 PM. They've been here for over half an hour already. He's beginning to get bored. He's taken in all the sights that can be taken in from here. What he'd really like to do is head on down to the docks and grab an early dinner. He's spotted some great restaurants. He's almost able to read the menus from some of them at his vantage point. They could be expensive, but that doesn't matter. NANA's paying.

Tom looks down and watches a seagull circling high above the water. Where he sits, above this gaping maw where Lisbon can't decide if it's drinking North Atlantic or regurgitating Tagus, the water is blue, shallow, and ocean. Off to his east he can see the muddy slurry of the river trying to empty its bowels into the toilet bowl of the North Atlantic.

A large cargo ship slides lazily underneath him. Tom yawns and tosses the last piece of his granola bar that was squirreled away in his pocket out toward the docks. It'll never get there. A seagull swoops in and catches it. He's impressed. It never got halfway down toward the water.

James Seaton is sitting on the other side of Maurice. He's made himself comfortable. He doesn't take the binoculars away from his eyes ever. He keeps scanning. He loves the cloak and dagger stuff. He's Maurice's eyes until they spot the three Iranians.

Tom looks at his watch again. His watch reads all the fours: 4:44 PM. Maybe they'll get a bingo. He's thinking he might just lean back against the beam of the bridge and catch some shuteye. But that would be tempting fate. He's not tied nearly securely enough to the bridge.

"I think I have them," says James.

He's looking down toward the docks. Tom raises his binoculars to his face, following the line that James's hand is pointing. He doesn't get them right away. He scans farther away and then he sees them. The three men in slacks and shirts. It's a warm day. They duck into a store and Tom loses them again. Then they reappear a few minutes later.

Maurice has located them with his binoculars. Now he's adjusting the sight on his rifle. It's a large rifle with a much bigger bore than regular sniper rifles. This one shoots a low velocity miniature rocket. It's about the size of his thumb, the rocket is. All he needs to do is lock it onto the target and pull the trigger.

The rocket will do most of the rest, depending upon the environment. There are many types of rockets that can be launched to deliver these vectors or nanobots. Indoors, Maurice prefers helis. In the outdoors, a rocket is more appropriate to mitigate against winds and outdoor airflow.

Maurice loads a rocket. Inside it carries a baker's dozen nanobots. Maurice is superstitious like that. Thirteen nanobots might seem like overkill, but you need a safety margin. It's like the sperm and the egg; only one gets in, but it takes millions to make the try.

"When do you want me tag them?" Maurice asks.

He's talking to James but he's looking through his site. The Iranians have disappeared into another store.

"Ideally," says James, "I'd like to see them taking a beverage or a bite at one of those outdoor patios."

James taps the earpiece in his ear. "Maggie?" he asks.

"Maggie here," comes the reply.

"Where are you?"

"Trailing the target, by the silk shop."

Tom scans with his binoculars and finds her. She's an attractive woman, fitting in just like a tourist. She's fondling a colored scarf.

"Gotcha," says James.

She looks up and winks toward the bridge. James sees it.

"Was that for me?"

"What?" she says.

"That wink."

"Oh, no. Sorry, James. I think I must have gotten something in my eye."

Tom laughs.

"I'm telling you, it was for me," James says to Tom.

"Or me," Tom replies.

"They're on the move again," says Maurice.

The three Iranians come out of the store and start heading away from them. Maggie slowly walks behind them, keeping a distance. They pass several stores. They stop at some of them, talk and gesticulate, but then move on. They'll soon be at the end of the run of shops along the docks.

"You want me to tag them?" asks Maurice again.

"No," says James, "I want them to sit down and take a load off. It's too hard to get a lock at this distance with all the other tourists around."

Maurice nods. He has a point. Moving targets are always harder to get a confirmed lock on.

"In any event, we have Maggie as boots on the ground. If we lose them she can transmit a lock for you and you can launch blindly," says James.

Maurice understands that but he doesn't like it. He doesn't want her stealing his thunder. He likes to be the one to tag 'em and bag 'em. It's more fun watching the whole dance of nano technology unfold in front of you.

The Iranians turn around at the end of the dock and stop. Maggie is looking at a magazine on a rack in front of her. She's wearing dark sunglasses and glances a look back at them.

"Can you hear what they're saying?" asks James.

"Not at the moment. But one of them was suggesting a restaurant earlier," Maggie replies.

There's more arm-waving and gesticulating and animated conversation. Dr. Saatchi is pointing down the docks from where they came. The two others nod their heads and they start walking back briskly.

At the first restaurant they come to, which happens to be opposite from where Maggie is standing, they stop. It has an outdoor patio. A waitress comes up to them and smiles. She says something. They respond. She shows them to a table under an umbrella, but at this angle, height, and distance the umbrella is not concealing them from the three NANA agents on the bridge.

"Move in," says James.

Maggie puts the magazine back in the rack and crosses over to the restaurant. The same waitress greets her and shows her to a seat. The three Iranians look at her as she walks past them. She smiles at them. Dr. Saatchi smiles back. Maggie is seated one table away.

The three Iranians are looking at menus. Maggie is handed one too and glances down at it.

"Okay," says James, "everyone is in place. Maurice, tag 'n' bag at your leisure."

Maurice adjusts his sites, and Gen. Najafi's face fills his site. He pushes a button on the side of his rifle. The general's face is identified and locked in. He does the same with Gen. Bukhari. But he can't get enough of a profile or even full-frontal of Dr. Saatchi's face for a locked-in ID.

"I need Maggie to take a lock on Saatchi," Maurice says to James.

"Maggie, we need Saatchi," James says.

Maggie still has her sunglasses on. She looks up and Saatchi is looking right back at her, smiling like a wolf. Maggie adjusts her sunglasses, at the same time taking a digital image of his smiling face. She gives him a curt smile back before looking back down at her menu. She clicks one of the buttons on her watch.

"Should be coming now," she whispers.

James looks at Maurice.

"I have confirmation," Maurice says.

"Good work," says James, speaking to Maggie.

In the site of his rifle, Maurice can see the computer streaming data and arming the nanobots. They'll be dropped from the rocket, looking and being the size of mosquitoes. They will inject each of the men with several smaller nanobots. The ones that Tom will connect with to end their lives.

Maurice gets confirmation that the nanobots are ready and armed. He squeezes the trigger. All he feels is a very light push on his shoulder as the rocket escapes out of the barrel.

James opens up his tablet and watches the rocket go as if he were riding on top of it. The rocket reaches the Iranians and hovers twenty feet above their heads. Little mosquitoes seem to drop out of its belly, and the rocket races off over the harbor where it skims along the water before self-destructing out of sight.

Saatchi gets up and comes over to stand by Maggie's table. She's just his type, though older than he would prefer.

"May I have a seat?" he asks, already pulling out a chair and smiling warmly.

"Sorry, no, I'm waiting for my husband."

His hand stops pulling back the chair and the smile on his face drops off. A mosquito buzzes around his neck and sinks its needle into his flesh. A dozen or more nanobots are released into his blood stream in a split second. Before he realizes he's been bitten, the nanobot disengages and drops to the floor where it self-destructs in a small puff of smoke. Hardly detectable to the human eye.

Reflexively, Dr. Saatchi smacks his neck but he is too late. The package has been delivered and there is nothing to be squashed under his palm. The same thing is happening almost in unison to Gen. Najafi and Bukhari.

"Damn mosquitoes," says Saatchi, more angrily than he needs to.

He walks back to his table and sits back down. He curses under his breath and then orders from the menu.

"We have confirmation, sir. All three packages have been delivered," says Maurice.

"Good work, everyone," says James. "I'm coming to rescue you."

He's talking to Maggie. He's going to pretend to be her husband. He'd like to have the benefits of that, but that isn't going to happen. This is work. And besides, she likes Tom the best.

Within an hour, the nanobots will be placed within the brain, ready to deliver their final EOL message to the unsuspecting Iranians.

JASON BLACKER

2:48 PM

Oval Office, The White House

Claude Martin walks into the secretary's office and over clean, tightly woven carpet that bears the seal of the president. The secretary gets up from behind her desk, knocks and pauses at the door to the office. Then she opens it and walks in. She is followed by Yolanda and Claude, who is admiring Yolanda's butt, just briefly and discreetly. It is, after all, one of the small mercies of being a gentleman.

"Mr. President," says the secretary, "Mr. Claude Martin and Ms. Yolanda Butts of NANA to see you."

President Towles is walking around his desk toward them. He is an old man. Sixty-eight and in bad shape. His face is ruddy and his nose the bulbous cauliflower of a man who enjoys too much liquor. It amazed Claude that this man had won the leadership of his party, but that he had gone on to win the presidency made him incredulous.

"How do you do?" asks President Towles, shaking Yolanda's hand and then Claude's in turn. "Please sit," he says, gesturing to the firm and uncomfortable couch that is across from and away from his large presidential desk.

Yolanda and Claude sit down. Claude is nervously hopeful about this meeting. It is the first one he has had with the incumbent president. In his briefcase he has a few dossiers of NANA's most successful wins, as well as many facts and figures as to why NANA needs a larger budget and how well that money will be spent.

Claude Martin is not frivolous with American taxpayers' money. He doesn't buy thousand dollar toilet seats or allow his agents unnecessary luxuries. Function must come first before form and fit. Even better if function can trump both form and fit.

His apartment is a sparse one-bedroom place, less than eight hundred square feet and appointed with the absolute essentials. He drives a small American sedan and he eats lunch most days at an American fast-food restaurant. He loves his country but he abhors waste and greed that the American people have fallen victim to. The current preside a perfect example.

Claude Martin makes a good six-figure salary as the head of a secret US government agency, but half his money goes back to charities of his choice. Mostly right-leaning political groups.

Claude feels prepared for this meeting, but he is unsure of President Towles stand on terrorism and how best to fight it.

President Towles takes a high-winged back chair across from the couch and across from a coffee table, which also carries the seal of the president. He sits a good foot taller than Claude and Yolanda. This is not by accident. President Towles looks at his two security agents. "Please give us a moment."

They walk outside and position themselves on either side of the door to the Oval Office. The president's secretary is busy typing at her terminal. She pays them no attention.

"So," begins President Towles, "tell me about this agency that nobody has heard of except the president. What do you call yourselves? NANA, a cute acronym for National Agency for Nano Agents. Is that correct?"

President Towles is looking at a sheet of paper before him that he had prepared. Claude nods his head. His face is the controlled slate sheet of a poker player. Claude is resting his hands on top of his briefcase which sits on his lap, just as it had when he was waiting outside. President Towles adjusts his glasses to better read his scrawl on the page before him.

"And you call your agents NINJAs. Nana Implanted Neurally Jammed Assassins, correct?" President Towles looks up and his fat face is being squashed to either side by a big grin. He takes his glasses off and puts them on the piece of paper now sitting on the coffee table. "Tell me what you'd like and what you need."

"Well, Mr. President, I'd first like to thank you for meeting with us. I know you are a very busy man," says Claude.

The President waves him off.

"If I might," says Claude, opening up his briefcase and taking out a couple of the dossiers, "I'd like to tell you a little more about what it is that we do in service of this great country of ours."

"I know what you do. You assassinate people while they sleep, without leaving a trace, without even being in the same room or city as they are. It's all very clever," says President Towles.

"Thank you, Mr. President," says Claude, taking what was meant as a backhanded slap like a compliment. "I'd like to tell you about one of our most recent high-profile cases that occurred just the other day, where we severed the ability of Iran to develop nuclear weapons. We've already eradicated the arms dealer Amaury Querry, and by tomorrow two top generals and a top nuclear physicist of the Iranian government will be no more."

"So, that was you who killed the Canadian?"

Claude nods, allowing himself a small smile and sense of pride.

"We can't have that," President Towles says. "We can't go around killing the civilians of our friends."

"But he was going to sell nuclear arms and technology to—"

President Towles puts his hand up to stop Claude from continuing. "I am the president now, and you'll play by my rules."

Claude stares at the president for a moment. His eyes flash hot like burning coals. He feigns a more pained smile and nods his head.

"Of course, Mr. President."

"The kind of work that we do, Mr. President," says Yolanda, trying to give Claude some time to recompose himself, "is delicate, discreet, and highly technological. As such, there are costs involved, especially in technology. But more than that, we'd like to expand. We can make America and her allies much safer if we have more agents at play at any time. The secret weapon in our program is that our enemies can never point the finger at the United States government as being responsible. We're never there at the scene."

President Towles nods his head. "I understand that. It is a great benefit of your work."

Yolanda reaches into the briefcase that is on Claude's lap and pulls out a folder labeled "Budget."

"Our budget is exceptionally small when you compare it to the CIA's for instance," Yolanda continues. "We have, I'm sure you'll agree, made incredible strides in the international arena toward global peace on a budget that is scarcely more than 10 percent of theirs."

"Closer to 15 percent Ms. Butts," says President Towles.

"Yes sir."

"What are you asking for?" asks President Towles.

Yolanda glances at Claude and he nods at her. She opens up the folder and scans it for a moment.

"I am very proud of the work we have accomplished on our small two billion dollar budget. If we could manage five billion we could change the political landscape of the world in less than a year."

She knows that she and Claude would be very happy with four billion as their new budget, but asking for five gives the president the ability to slash a billion dollars from them if he feels he needs the last word, and NANA is still off to the races.

Yolanda looks at the president, and Claude smiles thinly. She played their cards extremely well. Even if they only walked out of here with three billion, he'd still consider it a victory.

"Here is our proposed budget if you'd like to take a look, if you didn't have the chance earlier," says Yolanda, holding the closed folder toward the president. He waves her off.

"I have had a chance to review your proposed budget and I've had a look at your past years' budgets."

"This is where we go for the win," thinks Claude. "Thank you, Mr. President," he says.

"You might want to hold that thought."

Claude's face stiffens into a mask of granite. He's not sure he likes the sound of that.

"I've reviewed your budget and this is what's going to happen. I'm cutting your budget to one billion and folding it into the CIA's larger budget."

"But Mr. President," says Claude, "I must protest. Nobody knows about our agency, not even the CIA. As far as they know, I'm consulting for private firms."

"Very well," says President Towles. "You'll get your check from the Treasury deposited into your account, but you're getting one billion. I don't see how an agency such as yours needs more than that. You only have, what, seven agents to date?"

"Yes, but that's because it is extremely time consuming and expensive to train them. That's why we need more," says Claude.

"You're still a new agency and unproven. Yes, you've done good work, and that's the reason you're still alive. We'll reevaluate in one year, but honestly, Mr. Martin, I see no reason why your agency can't continue to contribute with a smaller leaner budget. Many departments are getting slashed. These are hard times and we all have to make sacrifices."

"He doesn't understand the first thing about sacrifices," thinks Claude.

Yolanda's color has taken on an ashen hue. Anger and resentment have chiseled lines into Claude's stone-set face.

"Mr. President, you are making a big mistake. The country needs NANA and what she can do for our country's long-term protection and safety," says Claude.

"Time will tell. You're still getting to run the show and you'll still be able to do your good work. But there is one other thing."

Claude can't bear to listen to this man speak anymore.

"You can go ahead with the assassination of these three Iranians, but from here on out, you'll do nothing without my prior verbal agreement."

Claude clenches his teeth. He wants to reach across the coffee table and shake this damn fool by the lapels. Claude has never before had to ask for permission, and he'll be damned if he starts now. He's not a child. He's the only man keeping Americans safe at night.

"Have I made myself clear?"

Claude swallows hard. He looks at the president with eyes that would cut him to ribbons if they were knives.

"Perfectly."

"That will be all then."

President Towles gets up and walks them to the door. As he shows them out he says, "So good of you to come. I expect weekly updates."

3:13 PM

The White House Parking Lot

Claude walks up to his ten-year-old Taurus. It's black in color and runs well. He smacks the hood of it and climbs into the driver's seat.

"This is the thanks we get for our service and loyalty to the country," he thinks.

This is his own private car. He bought it when it was three years old so that he wouldn't have to deal with the depreciations. This is how he watches his money, and it's also how he watches the taxpayers' money too. The only extravagance coming out of his office is the technology. But that's a necessity.

He got the Taurus as a gift for himself when he started NANA. It was a splurge, at least by his standards. But it served him well and it didn't cost the taxpayers a nickel, other than the cost of his salary, which back then was a modest, mid-five figures. In fact, he'd taken a substantial pay cut, almost half, to start NANA from the ground up.

One hundred and eighty thousand miles on his ten-year-old Taurus. Regular tune-ups and upkeep and it still runs well. You can count on American engineering and manufacturing when they get it right. He figures he'll get another five years out of this car easily. He'll get a quarter million miles out of his baby. He knows he will.

And he uses his own damn car. Not like those CIA assholes who get a new lease every three years. Only the best for those Crappy Intelligence Assholes. And now they're doing a pilot where they're buying Japanese vehicles. Not that he's got anything against the Japanese—his favorite agent is Japanese-American—but if you're spending taxpayers' money, you ought to keep it at home.

Yolanda stops by the passenger door and takes a big breath. She's got to prepare herself; she knows Claude is gonna go off. Not at her, but she's his sounding board. She's pissed too, but what can you do. When the president makes an executive decision, you've gotta deal with it. Roll with the punches, like her father used to say.

She'll bring Claude down from the cliff like she has before, but this is going to be a tough one. Neither of them expected that they'd see their budget cut. Good thing Claude is so damn stingy with money. He'll still be able to keep the teams they have up and running. At least for the first six months.

Yolanda opens up the passenger door and slides into her seat. She closes the door like she's at the library. She doesn't want to encourage the bear. She's learned that it's best not to speak before Claude starts. It's only worse if you try and start out soft with him.

"That fucking guy!" he says. "Who does he think he is?"

The president of the United States. But she doesn't say that. She only thinks it. She didn't vote for him. She doesn't think that Claude did either, but still, the people did and it is the people they serve. Claude is always telling her that. "We're servants of the good people of the USA. And our job is to protect them from evil so they can go about their business."

She'd heard that speech umpteen times. She could hear it in her mind, clear as if he was saying it to her right now. And she admires him for it. His patriotism and his dedication to building NANA into the best secret spy agency that the US had ever had. And he was doing it with nobody knowing about it.

Claude smacks the steering wheel not once, not twice, but several times. Yolanda wasn't counting. She is looking out the front window. She can barely see the North Lawn Fountain from where she is. The White House is in front of her and to her right. They are parked along West Executive Avenue.

Claude has grabbed the steering wheel with both his hands and he is shaking it vigorously. More realistically, it looks like he is being electrocuted by the thing. His teeth are clenched and his wispy thin hair is a messy tangled brown nest.

"Can you believe that cocksucker?" he asks Yolanda rhetorically.

She doesn't mind his tantrums; they're rare. Usually he is the example of fastidious quiet resolve and decorum. But when he has a tantrum, as Yolanda likes to call them, his language is more colorful than any sailor she's met.

"I can't fucking believe it. That guy. That fucking guy!"

Claude is literally frothing at the mouth. His spittle is bubbly and white at the corners of his mouth. Yolanda thinks this is her time to enter the conversation. Claude has strung more than one sentence together. He's starting to think.

"I can't believe it, Claude. I honestly can't. There was no way in hell that we were coming out of there with less money. No way."

Claude has stopped vibrating, but his knuckles are still white like marble gripping the steering wheel. This whole time the two of them haven't looked at each other. Both are staring out the front windshield looking yonder across the lawn.

"He didn't give us the scheduled hour. He was late and he didn't even look at any of the documents we had. More than that, he was abrasive and he cut us off well before our time was scheduled to end. Two thirty to three thirty. That's what we had been allotted. It's important business we had for him."

Claude looks at his watch again. It's just gone three twenty. "It's still not even three thirty."

Yolanda is pleased with how quickly Claude is coming down from the cliff. It's always a good sign when he stops swearing.

"What are we going to do?" Yolanda asks, turning to look at him.

Claude grits his teeth and furrows his brow. He knows what has to be done. You can't work with a man who has no patriotism in his heart. A man who lacks true leadership and vision.

"We need a new president," he says, still looking through the windshield.

His knuckles are now turning pink. He's relaxing his grip on the steering wheel. No longer is he wrapped up in a ball of anger and vitriol. No, Claude has bounced back; he always bounces back. When everything is black around you, you just have to give it a moment and the light will come in. Illumination will prevail. Just as it has now.

Yolanda laughs out loud. And she laughs again. Claude looks at her. He's not laughing. In fact, he's his cool, calm, and collected self. She stops laughing and looks at him, searching his eyes for any sign of insincerity. There is none.

"We need a new president," he says again, this time directly to her.

"But...but I don't understand."

"You will," he says.

He turns on the ignition. He feels like a calm glacial lake as he backs the car out of the parking stall and heads toward the exit. Americans deserve a president who will protect them. A man who has a vision, a man who is a true patriot. Claude is certain the VP is that kind of a man. The boozehound needs to go.

4:07 AM

Lisbon, Portugal

Inside a small hotel room in the inner city, Tom is sitting and watching a Portuguese show on TV. It has no subtitles and he can't tell what the hell is going on. But it's something to pass the time with.

This hotel is dingy and run-down. It's not in the touristy part of town, but it'll have to do. It will do. James received word earlier that their budget was a hundred bucks for the night. For two rooms. Did they have any idea how hard it was to find a hotel room in Lisbon on that kind of chump change?

But that's how Claude is. He is excruciatingly budget-conscious. But this is just over the top. Anthony didn't give him any insight as to the change, but he figured out the reasons all by himself. Claude was supposed to meet the president earlier according to rumor inside NANA. Guess that didn't go so well.

The four of them are inside Tom's room. Well, Tom's and Maurice's room. But right now it isn't a hotel room; it is central ops. James and Maggie are sitting at the table. It barely has enough space to hold Maggie's computer. Beside her is a large metal box, about the size of a suitcase. This is the smallest size the technology can be made and still be effective in communicating between the nanobots inside target and agent. It is heavy, over fifty pounds, but it works great.

She can't understand how the technology could develop nanobots the size of single cells and yet the equipment needed to run them are the size of houses...almost.

James is trying to play solitaire, but Maggie's oversized laptop is taking up more space. He gives up and starts shuffling the cards and trying to figure out how to do a card trick he learned once, many years ago.

Maurice is sitting on the couch next to Tom, sipping a local beer. His feet are on the table and he is relaxing. His work is done for this portion of the job, and he would like to get some shut-eye, but that isn't going to happen until Tom finishes his work.

Tom is sipping on a glass of water that is blistering sweat. His eyes are heavy. What with the jet lag and the uneventful day and the time of morning it is, he is well past his prime. If these Iranians didn't go to bed recently, he's pretty sure they would have pulled the plug on tonight's kill.

But the Iranians did go to bed, at just after 3:00 AM, but they haven't yet entered REM.

Maggie knows the swanky hotel they are in. One of the few five-star hotels in Lisbon. She doesn't know it intimately but she has been inside and looked around. The Iranians each have their own room. Well, that isn't really true; each of the Iranians has his own suite. Of course, Dr. Saatchi brought a high-priced hooker up to his room earlier. He didn't beat her, but he was rough. She was long gone by now.

Gen. Bukhari said his prayers and took a long bath before retiring for the night. Gen. Najafi all but emptied the in-room bar and he fell on the bed in a drunken stupor, shortly after Bukhari had gone to bed.

Maggie doesn't like that. The fact that Najafi is in an alcohol-induced sleep doesn't bode well for his assassination. REM sleep is terribly unreliable in drunks. If she were to place a wager, she'd say that Najafi would be the last extermination of Tom's tonight. First up, she figures, will be the serene and peaceful Bukhari. She is wrong.

On her computer screen she gets confirmation that Saatchi has entered REM.

"Tom," she says, "we have REM on Saatchi."

Tom gets up and undresses to his boxer briefs and goes and lies down on the bed, which will be his to actually sleep in if he ever gets the chance.

"Do you need help? You look awfully tired," says Maggie.

"I could use a pick-me-up. I'm not certain I'll be able to enter Theta and not fall asleep myself."

"Sure," she says.

Maggie opens up a small briefcase-sized case, which contains an assortment of pharmaceuticals, most of which are not available to the public.

She looks for something that will act like a mild amphetamine. But you can't use amphetamines during such sensitive meditative work because it will prevent the agent from reaching the deep meditative state during which they can eliminate their objectives.

She finds what she was looking for. It is a bottle that contains a clear liquid. It is labeled "Somgilant," a portmanteau of somnolence and vigilant. It does pretty much what those two words suggest. It allows for peaceful, vigilant maintenance of Theta brain states in otherwise fatigued agents. It hasn't been used on humans before, but all computer models suggest it will work terrifically.

Tom knows the risks. That is why he hardly ever wants to use the pharms.

"This will help you keep active and alert while deep in Theta. It will also help maintain Theta," says Maggie.

Maggie finds a vein in Tom's wrist and attaches an IV of saline fluids. These pharms have to be dosed just right. She knows his weight; he's 138 pounds soaking wet. She does a quick calculation in her mind. Tom will need a 6.6 mL dose off the bat with maintenance of 1.4 mL consistently dripped during each half hour.

"What's it called?" he asks.

"Somgilant," she says, smiling at him.

He grins at her, and she looks deep into his eyes before looking back at attaching the drug to the IV.

"How comforting," he says.

James comes over dragging the large heavy suitcase of equipment. He opens it up for Maggie. It is self-powered but she has him plug it in just to be sure. She turns it on and a variety of colored lights blink, cycle through their startup, and then stay steady. She attaches electrodes all over him.

"Okay, you're good to go," she says, patting his upper arm.

She heads back to the table and pulls up a screen of his vitals.

"Are we still good?" asks James.

Maggie nods. Saatchi is still in REM. Tom can feel the effects of the drug almost immediately. He feels relaxed and curiously awake at the same time. "This is going to be too easy," he thinks to himself. He enters into meditation, drifting into the deeper brainwave stages, easily and comfortably as if he were sinking into warm honey.

"Tom's in Theta," Maggie says, looking at her computer screen. "That was quick," she thinks.

She watches him, his deep breathing and his smooth, sinewy muscled physique. She wants to lie down with him and feel his heartbeat under her ear. She's not sure she'll ever get the chance. Claude frowns on interoffice romance of any kind, and she's not even sure Tom likes her.

Tom finds himself looking into a mirror. It takes a moment for him to find his bearings. He appears to be naked and his face is painted with war paint so it seems. He takes a moment to steady himself and take in the scene. It slowly comes more into focus. He's a woman, an attractive woman with blonde hair and lots of makeup.

He's on his hands and knees and he can see his silicon-enhanced breasts in the mirror. His ass is up in the air and behind him is Saatchi. He's naked and hairy and he's fucking Tom. Saatchi is drooling at the corner of his mouth. He reaches down beside him and picks up a belt. Saatchi swings it down across Tom's back.

It doesn't sting because he isn't really here, but the body he's inhabiting gives out a squeal. Saatchi does this again and again until he finally orgasms.

Tom feels violated even though he's not really here. He's tired of ending up as women in these other men's dreams and he's eager to kill Saatchi right away here. He takes a look at Saatchi's head just to confirm he's the target. The red beacon starts small and pulsates into a huge angry-looking zit taking up most of his head. They're the only two in this room of Saatchi's dream, but still, protocol says you have to get visual confirmation.

As Saatchi finishes his orgasm, he takes the belt and pulls it over and around Tom's head. He yanks on it hard. This is not a good sign. If Saatchi manages to kill this woman—Tom—in this dream, Tom will end up dead in real life. Though he figures Maggie is on it and will pull him out before that happens. Still, the threat is real, and more than that, he hasn't got much time to kill Saatchi either before he blacks out.

Tom reaches up with one hand and pulls at the inside of the leather belt on the left side of his neck. He takes his hand and yanks down hard on the belt. It opens up just enough to bring blood coursing back into his head.

Down on the floor at the end of the bed, Tom can see this woman's high heeled stilettos. They have a blunt but metallic point. If only he could reach them. He can't. He stretches his fingers, red with nail polish, out toward them. This hand, these slender female fingers reach like wriggling worms, but they're not long enough. Saatchi is leaning back with all his might, holding onto the two ends of the leather belt like he's riding a bucking bronco.

Tom figures he can't fight the man like this. He brings his right hand back onto the bed, and with all his might, he pushes with this one hand and both knees back toward Saatchi.

Saatchi is taken by surprise and Tom feels the belt go slack. Saatchi tumbles backward off the bed and Tom falls after him. A side table is broken and falls to pieces as Saatchi's robust physique lands on it. Tom lands upon him and tries to get a good elbow into the man's side, but these are not his arms and he hasn't full acclimatized to this body. The elbow is stopped by Saatchi's ribs, not having the effect he intended.

Tom is on the side of the bed opposite to where the stilettos are. He scrambles onto his hands and knees and starts crawling around the end of the bed when his foot gets caught by something.

"Come here, you slut," says Saatchi in his thick accent.

"Fuck you," says Tom in the woman's voice.

He kicks at the clutching hand with his other foot and the hand lets go. Tom scurries along. He's almost around the other side of the bed when Saatchi grabs him and pulls him up to standing.

Tom is now looking at this big hairy man. Saatchi stands almost a foot taller than this woman's body he's in.

"You stupid American whore," says Saatchi.

And Tom is intrigued by that because the woman didn't sound American. She sounded British when she told him to fuck off.

Saatchi backhand slaps her across the face.

"I'm going to kill you, American slut," he says.

Tom reaches for the man's groin and grabs a small mound of soft flesh and hair. He twists it hard. Saatchi jumps up and back, screaming in pain. He's backing away and Tom uses this opportunity to bend down and reach for the stiletto.

Saatchi is quicker than his thick frame would suggest. He recovers quickly from shock and injury. He grabs Tom's long blonde hair and yanks on it hard. Toms head is yanked back, but his fingers find the stiletto.

"Now you're going to pay, you American pig whore," says Saatchi.

Tom spins around and slams the end of the stiletto's heel into Saatchi's soft temple.

"I am not an American whore," he says in the woman's British voice, slamming the stiletto back into the side of Saatchi's face, again and again.

"I am a British slut."

He's surprised by that. He usually prefers "courtesy of Hattori Hanzo" as the last words his target hears, but for some reason, he either got into character too much, or this woman in Saatchi's dream just needed to have the last word. Either way, he looks down at Saatchi's bloodied face, and slowly everything fades out.

"EOL confirmed," says Maggie. "That was a close one. His vitals went quite erratic for a moment there. I thought we might have to pull him out."

James nods and grunts. Maurice finishes his beer and pulls another out of the mini bar.

1:01 PM

A Professional Building, Washington DC

Claude sits at his desk in his office. These offices, the small three thousand square feet, are the head offices of NANA. Though that's not what it says on the door. The door has a placard upon which is inscribed "Fleming, Greene and Le Carré, LLC."

The lease is paid for by a shell company called Fleming, Greene and Le Carré, LLC. Claude thought it was quite clever at the time. Hiding in plain sight, so to speak. Most people get Fleming. Who wouldn't? Many others get Le Carré, but Claude can count on one hand the people who get all three right.

Fleming, Greene and Le Carré bills itself as a lobby group. Under that cover, it allows Claude and his team to visit the White House often as needed.

Claude's desk is sparse. There is a three-level tray that holds a few wisps of papers, and in front of him on his desk is a large desk calendar. It is open to the current month. There are only a few scribbles on it, cryptic scratchings that only Claude understands.

Behind him is a shelf of books. There are many spy novels on it, as well as political books and biographies. Nothing that seems out of the ordinary for a lobbyist's office.

Across from the desk is a 3.5 by 3.5 foot print of Norman Rockwell's Homecoming Marine. On the right wall, right as you enter Claude's office, is a 40 x 30 inch print of John Singleton Copley's Watson and the Shark.

Some might argue that Copley wasn't truly American, but those arguing wouldn't win. Claude considers him American, and he was, born in Boston. That is good enough. America is in his blood. That Copley spent his later years in England is irrelevant.

Besides, Watson and the Shark speaks to Claude. In this political capital, he is surrounded by sharks, and having that painting within eyesight reminds him of it. Claude gets up and takes a look at it. It is a multi-racial America helping the weak, the naked, the vulnerable. That's what NANA does. Claude smiles and strokes the harpoon held precariously above the shark.

He is that harpoon. The tip of the spear, and he relishes his position, his hidden and cloaked position, as the first line of defense for the American people.

Claude walks back to his desk and sits down again. He steeples his fingers in front of him and looks off to his right, out the window. If you enter Claude's office, the first thing you might detect is the faint smell of smoke.

Just under Claude's desk to the right is a steel trashcan. Its insides are smeared with black carbon. It is empty now. It gets emptied at the end of each day. Papers that Claude feels are too important to keep "live" get burned. Behind him, also to his right is a shredder. A cross-cut shredder that shreds to a quarter of an inch.

This shredder is also empty. It gets emptied at the end of each day too. Important papers get shredded first before being burned, and they get shredded with other random printed material on a one-to-one basis.

Files that are needed are kept securely in a biometric accessible safe that only he and Yolanda have access to. When a job has been completed, all files related to it are shredded and burned. The only known memory of any events NANA has been involved with is kept in a small diary with cryptic characters and numbers indicating the event, the number involved, who was erased and so forth.

Claude has an eidetic memory. It has served him well. As much as some have accused him of previous indiscretions, nobody has found evidence of them. And they never will. The only evidence of anything he's ever been involved with are the diaries he keeps. And only he knows where they're kept. Claude allows no computers at NANA's head offices, except for the odd laptop that controllers might need to bring in. Perhaps he is paranoid, but he finds them notoriously unreliable and accessible even with so-called encryptions and irrevocable erasure methods.

Claude puts his mind to the problem with the president. It weighs him down. Never before has he had to deal with an unpatriotic American, and that his unpatriotic American is the president upsets Claude. One billion dollars means that NANA is on life support. It's barely enough to keep current projects going.

The president might just have castrated him and asked him to sire offspring. That's what this feels like to Claude. It is a sucker punch to the solar plexus. But the worst part is having to run any activity by the president. That has never happened before. President Larrison trusted him, as he should have. And Claude was damned if he was going to allow an unpatriotic boozer of a president dictate which matters and activities were best for national security.

He has tried to reason with the president, but it seems Towles is an unreasonable man. But VP Matney, she seems like a reasonable, true blue patriot. Claude reasons he could work with her. She seems more hands-off, more trusting of those who have been entrusted with the welfare and security of the American people.

Claude grits his teeth. What he needs to do, for the good of America and her citizens, is not something he relished. But it has to be done. He reaches for his phone and dials Yolanda.

"Can I see you," he says, and then he puts down the phone.

A minute later there is a knock at the door.

"Come in," he says.

Yolanda comes in and smiles at him. She walks up to the desk.

"Please sit down," he says.

She takes a seat across from him.

"What is it, Claude?" she asks.

She can see the worry drawn tight across his face. Claude looks out the window again and then back at her. He rests his forearms on his desk, clasping his hands. His arms are an arrow pointing at Yolanda. This is going to be her biggest test of faith and loyalty in him yet. But Claude is not intimidated. All those who work at NANA, all of them—well, except for him—have nanobots implanted and he knows the kill code.

Trust and loyalty are all well and good when earned and offered freely, but there is something to be said for having a backup plan. Always have a backup plan. Claude smiles at Yolanda.

"You and I go back many years."

Yolanda nods. "Almost fifteen years now."

Claude shakes his headed slowly and whistles. "Wow, we're like family."

Yolanda smiles.

"You know I trust you, Yola. We've been through some tough stuff together these fourteen, almost fifteen years."

"That's true. And I trust you, Claude. You took a chance on me when nobody else would."

"And I'm glad I did."

Claude isn't sure how best to approach this delicate subject. He believes he can trust her, but he will have to watch her closely for any tells.

"We're about to embark on a very dangerous, very difficult, and world-altering mission," he said.

Yolanda looks at him carefully before speaking. Her eyes narrow. "That's why I signed up. Our work is God's work."

And it is in God she trusts, and Claude. She believes he is truly inspired by God. He is a servant of God, she is sure of it. Claude smiles at her. He does feel inspired by God, even if he didn't quite believe in it.

"What if I told you we had to save America by sacrificing an American?"

Yolanda holds his gaze. "Then that is a sacrifice we would have to make."

"What if that American was the president?"

Claude holds his gaze on Yolanda. She swallows and her eyes flicker, but she doesn't look away. Claude likes that. It is a good sign. "A wolf can appear in sheep's clothing. Only the wise can tell."

"You would trust me then?"

"I would trust you to the ends of the earth."

Claude smiles. It is a somber smile. The work before them is difficult and dangerous, as he said. Assassinating the president is not something he considered lightly.

"Good," he says. "I want you to speak to R&D and have them develop some nanobots for me. I want it put in a fragile shell that can be easily broken underfoot and that will disappear once broken."

Yolanda nods.

"You understand what's at stake here, Yola?"

"Yes," she says. "If the king must be sacrificed to save the queen, then it must be done. You can trust me."

She doesn't like the idea of assassinating the president, but she was at the meeting with Claude. She found President Towles to be unreasonable and arrogant. He seems to be unsympathetic, maybe even downright treasonous. She will stand by Claude as he stood by her all these years. It's not like he is attempting a coup. He is looking out for America's best interests.

"America and the world will be a safer place for it," he says.

She nods. "I believe you."

4:27 AM

Lisbon, Portugal

Tom is coming out of his meditation where he erased Saatchi. He prefers dreams where he has at least some way of choosing which actor he will play in it. But when there's only one other person in a target's dreams, well, that's the person you have to be.

Tom slips his feet off the side of the bed. He feels energized but also serene. "A guy could get used to a drug like this," he thinks.

"EOL confirmed?" he asks.

Maggie nods. "Yeah, but we were worried about you there for a moment. I thought I'd have to pull you out."

Tom smiles. "Me too. I woke up in his dream as a hooker on all fours. Not exactly how I would have preferred to enter his dreamscape." He shakes his head. "That's two in a row now that I've been woman. Perhaps I have mommy issues," he says.

Maggie laughs and Maurice almost spilled his beer all over himself. Maggie's laptop starts beeping again.

"Don't get too comfortable," Maggie says. "Looks like we have Najafi in REM. Are you good to go?"

"I am," says Tom as he lies back down.

"Be careful this time," Maggie says.

Tom doesn't say anything. He is well on his way into Theta brainwave meditation states. Maggie taps into her laptop as she has done dozens of times before. She is aligning Tom's nanobot with Najafi's, otherwise Tom might randomly connect to anyone with a nanobot within a radius of up to a thousand miles. At least, that is the potential. Not a good connection, but it can be done.

Tom saw a painting once of hell. At least, one artist's interpretation of hell. The scene as he recalls was in dark oranges, reds, and blacks. It was mostly barren with raging fires dotted along the ground. Smoke was thick and acrid, and there was a picture of the classic two-horned devil. The devil had a forked tongue and a pointed tail. Well, Tom has just awoken into such a scene. A horrific nightmare, the likes of which turn his stomach.

Tom looks at himself. He is a naked old man. Thin, and his skin sags across the wire hangers that are his skeleton. His hands are clasped behind him, and he is being held under each arm by red devils the same size as him. They look just like the devil he had seen in the painting. With forked tongues, pointed tails, two horns on their heads, and cloven feet like horses.

Tom looks around. He is being dragged toward a large fat man who looks like the smiling Buddha's evil twin. He is five times the size of Tom. He is red and fat and his teeth are pointing like arrows.

Tom is third in a line of men, women, and children who are being dragged toward this massive devil. Tom sees him take the first man who is now up. The smaller devils release him to the large Buddha, and this evil monstrosity tears the man in two and tosses each half of his body into separate pits of bubbling lava. One pit is on the left side and the other is on the right.

Tom looks around and finds his target. Sitting next to this evil Buddha is a black dog that looks mangy and hungry with burning red eyes. The dog is slobbering and it has no teeth. Its head pulses the blue beacon that grows and then retreats and repeats itself.

Deep within his meditative state, Tom transfers himself into the evil Buddha. It is like imagining smoke being blown from his current avatar to the avatar he wants to be—the Buddha. He exhales white smoke from his mouth and enters the nostrils of the evil Buddha, and in the next moment he is looking down at the line in front of him. It stretches as far as the eye can see. Next up is a small girl. She is naked, as they all are, and Tom knows that as the evil Buddha, he is about to pick her up and rip in her two.

He can't stomach the thought. Instead, he reaches down to his left where the black mangy dog, his target, sits at his side, and he picks the dog up and rips Najafi in two and throws each half into the separate pits of bubbling lava.

"Courtesy of Hattori Hanzo," says Tom, but the voice is that of a deep, growling devil. Within seconds, everything disappears and Tom is lying on the bed, just deep in meditation.

"EOL confirmed," says Maggie. "He's on his A game tonight."

She likes to think that the Somgilant is of great help in Tom's abilities tonight. But she knows that he is a lethal and competent assassin both in life and dreams.

"Good," says James. "What about Bukhari? Is he ever going to drift into REM?"

It is a rhetorical question, but as he asks it, Maggie's laptop beeps again.

"Speak of the devil," she says. "Bukhari has just gone under."

"He's entered REM?" asks James.

Maggie nods. Tom is just bringing himself out of Theta meditation. His eyes flicker open and he looks over at them. Assassinations of this sort take their toll, both physically and emotionally. They are harder than real-life assassinations because of the effects they have on brain chemistry.

"Tom," says Maggie, "we need you to get back down there."

Maggie is sitting on the edge of the bed. She is taking his pulse, which is erratic. Tom seems weakened by these last two assassinations.

"Only if you're up for it," she says.

Concern is etched across her forehead in worried lines. Tom nods. "Might as well go for a hat trick."

"Be careful," she says.

Maggie returns to the table where James is still sitting. Maurice is watching late night television with the volume off. Peace and quiet are the order of this early morning if Tom is to complete a hat trick. James looks at Maggie as she sits back down.

"Don't worry about it. He'll be fine," says James.

Maggie looks at him and feigns a fragile smile. "No one has ever completed a hat trick before," she says. "We don't know the toll it will take on his mental and physical state. There's a reason we usually send in teams for this sort of thing."

"He's the best," says James. "If anyone can pull it off, Tom can."

Maggie isn't so sure. She is glad he took the pharms—that will help—but they aren't without their side effects. Side effects she isn't sure she wants to find out about.

She looks at his vitals and watches them carefully as she taps away at her laptop, connecting him with Bukhari. His respiration is high and his heart is beating like a galloping horse. She isn't going to allow this continue for too long.

The scene before Tom has bright, light browns and baby blues. He takes a moment to adjust. He is in the desert somewhere. There are no clouds in the sky, and the sun is burning down upon him like a lit cigarette. He looks at himself. He is dressed in white, a long flowing thawb, and on his head he feels a keffiyeh.

Tom is walking toward a group of people under a large white canopy that is protecting them from the sun. A young boy is running toward him.

"Abbi, Abbi," the boy is shouting.

He is dressed as Tom is, and his arms are outstretched for an embrace. The boy is handsome and his mouth is a big grin. He runs hard and fast and leaps into Tom's arms.

Tom can't help but pick him up and swing him around.

"Where are your mother and sister?" Tom asks.

The boy points back toward the canopy. Tom puts him down and holds his hand as they walk back toward the shelter.

"It's my birthday next week, Daddy," says the young boy.

"I know it is. How old will you be, Armin?"

And Tom looks down at this small boy walking hand in hand next to him. And he sees the blue beacon pulsing from inside his head, growing bigger and bigger and then smaller and smaller again. Tom swallows hard. He has never killed a boy before, not in dreams and certainly not in life.

"Six years old, Daddy."

"A big six-year-old boy," said Tom.

They walk in silence back toward the shelter. When they reach it, the wife stands up and offers Tom some water from a canteen.

"I have some sfiha for you," she says. "Come and eat."

Tom sits down next to his daughter and she smiles at him, putting her hand around his waist. He kisses her on the forehead. She appears to be a couple of years older than her brother, Armin. His wife serves him up the sfiha, a small open-faced pizza with ground lamb on it. It is cold.

Tom eats it with his left hand, and with his right he leans back, brushing against his Janbiya. He pulls it out and looks at its curved and sharp edges. He could so easily thrust this dagger into the little boy's heart. The thought makes him feel sick. He almost brings up the sfiha he just swallowed.

Tom looks at Armin. The blue beacon pulses continuously. The boy looks up at him still smiling.

"When can I have one?" asks Armin, pointing at the Janbiya in Tom's hand.

"When you are fourteen," says Tom.

Armin looks down at his fingers and starts counting with them, his mouth open and mouthing the numbers.

"Eight years time," Armin says. "That's too long."

"It will come quickly enough," says Tom.

Tom puts the dagger back in its sheath and ruffles Armin's mop of black hair. He has great feelings of love and tenderness for this young boy. It is strange. Usually he doesn't feel strong emotions in any of the dreams he enters. Perhaps it is the strength of the dreamer's emotions, Bukhari's emotions. Perhaps this is how Bukhari felt toward his own father when he was a boy.

In any event, it is upsetting Tom because it makes it harder for him to do his work. He needs to eradicate this target and deal with the threat. It's just that he has never had a target that was a boy.

He knows this was a dream. This really isn't a boy in front of him, yet it is still hard. Yes, it might be a dream, but this eradication is still real and it feels real. The plunging of the knife or the seeping of the blood. These always seem as real in dreams to Tom as they do in life.

"Perhaps when the boy turns around, or maybe if he takes a nap, I'll be able to do it," thinks Tom. He looks at the boy. Armin is stuffing his face with sfiha. Tom fingers the knife handle. It doesn't feel right. It doesn't feel comfortable in his hands, and it always does.

"Tea, my husband," says the wife.

She hands him a cup of tea. It is green and minty and sweet. Tom drinks from it; it is lukewarm. It is a sweet, minty green tea, the kind he's had in Morocco before. Armin turns around from Tom and faces away from him.

The boy is slim, and Tom can almost see his ribs through the thin cotton thawb he wears. Tom puts his hand on the Janbiya and pulls it halfway out of its sheath. He sees the boy's breathing. His back expands and contracts rhythmically with each breath. Tom tightens his grip on the handle. He knows exactly where the blade should enter. It would slip easily between the two ribs, through the lung, and puncture the heart.

If Tom is quick about it, the boy will barely feel a thing before he is dead. And the dagger's blade is long enough. These thoughts should comfort Tom, but they don't. His hand feels like a lead weight and he can't pull the dagger out of its sheath.

He's watching the boy's breathing, when a loud crack catches his attention. A split second later, there's a puff of sand a few feet to his right. Tom looks up. A couple of hundred feet away, three men on camels are riding toward them fast. They all have rifles.

Another crack, another puff of sand. This time closer, just a foot away. They're exposed. This is a problem for Tom. He's got to get out of this dream, but he can't. He feels he needs to protect the boy. It's strange, but he feels very paternal toward him.

Tom looks around. There are some old bags that contain their food and the canopy, but other than that, there's nothing here to protect them from the onslaught. Crack, searing pain. Tom looks down at his left shoulder. He's been hit by a bullet, a flesh wound. The thawb is absorbing the blood. The pain is hot and intense.

He's in Theta right now. He's done this dozens and dozens of times, if not hundreds, practicing and perfecting. He can manipulate the dream. He can make use of what some call lucid dreaming.

That's his only chance. If he doesn't do something or get out of the dream, he'll be dead. The flesh wound is just a wake-up call. He thinks, "What can I do?" There's just sand all around him.

And that's when it hits him.

"Lie down!" he yells to his family.

And suddenly, large sandbags are lining themselves in front of them. One row high, then two, three, four, five, and six. The bullets are hitting the sandbags. Tom can hear the soft pelting of the bullets at the sand. Like sand clogs against brick walls.

Tom looks around. The girl and the boy are lying down. Both of them are crying. The wife is lying between, her hands each over one of the children. She's scared, but she's trying to be brave for the children.

The sandbag wall is only about three feet high or so. Tom peeks over it, and as he does, a man jumps off the camel and jumps over the sandbags. His rifle is pointing in front of him, but he's just off to Tom's right. Tom unsheathes the Janbiya and he catches the man in midair. The knife enters quickly and quietly into his belly, and Tom uses it as a handle to throw the man forward over his head. The knife bites and chews deeper into his belly. The man screams in pain.

Just behind Tom, a second man has leapt over the sandbags. He comes up quickly behind Tom and cracks him over the head with the butt of the rifle.

Tom sees stars.

"Shit," he thinks to himself. "This might be the end."

Then the lights go out and everything is dark.

"I've gotta pull him out, now!" yells Maggie.

There's a look of panic on her face. Tom's vitals are off the charts.

"Do it," says James.

Maurice has come up and he's standing behind Maggie. He's looking over her shoulder and he can see that things don't look good. He doesn't understand it, but the red beeps, the blips, and the jagged lines are fast and chaotic. Any idiot could tell it wasn't good news.

Maggie taps fast on her laptop, her fingers whirring. Sweat starts to bead on her forehead. She has never seen it this bad. "Tom could die any second now," she thinks. She's trained for this. NANA has made sure they've all been trained for all sorts of black swan events. This isn't supposed to happen, but just in case it does, here's how you fix it. She's on autopilot, tapping away, trying to extract Tom from the dreamscape.

It's all automatic, thank God for the training. But something's wrong. Tom's not coming out. The messages are either getting ignored or not reaching him through the nanobot.

Maybe the nanobot has self-destructed. But that shouldn't make a difference. They implant over a dozen in the agents just for this type of redundancy. Computer models indicated that with the amount of redundancy involved, the chances of not being able to extricate an agent in this type of scenario are more than one in one septillion. In other words, it should be impossible not to extricate an agent.

"Get him out!"

Now James is yelling. He's looking over at Tom, and Tom is not looking good. He's twitching and moaning. His eyes open and flicker and then shut.

"I'm trying, goddammit, I'm trying. He's not responding," says Maggie.

Maggie glances up at him. He's not looking good at all. He could go into cardiac arrest at any second. Why won't the damn bots respond? They should have severed the connection already. He should be up talking to them. He should be smiling at them, at her, asking if the EOL was confirmed.

She taps away. She's trying different codes, sending different algorithms, but nothing is working. Tom's heartbeat stops. She looks at the screen, not believing it for a split second.

"Shit," she says. "He's gone into cardiac arrest."

She jumps up and runs over to the bed. Tom is lying still, he's not breathing, he's not moving.

"Get the electrodes off him! Just yank them off!"

James and Maurice start pulling them off. Maggie runs back to the table where she grabs her small bag of pharms. She starts pulling vials of medications out. She can't find the one she likes. At the bottom of the bag, of course, at the bottom of the damn bag, she finds it. The vial whose label says "Resusinate."

If they're going to bring him back, this'll do it or nothing will. She looks for a heavier gauge needle. A long one. She has to go directly into his heart. No heartbeat means she can't use the IV bag. She hates doing this; thank God he's unconscious.

Maggie finds the syringe and the needle. She attaches the needle to the syringe and pulls in 10 mL from the vial. She sits on the side of the bed.

"Hold him tight by the shoulders," she says.

James and Tom take a shoulder each and hold him down tight. Maggie counts the ribs and measures off the sternum. She has one chance, and she has to get this right. She plunges the needle in and empties the syringe. The effect she wants should happen within a few seconds.

7:37 PM

Run Down Industrial Plant, Outside Washington, D.C.

Claude parks his black Taurus in the dirt parking lot. There are no cars here. The cars and some trucks, all American—that was part of the deal to get hired here—are underground, around back. Though you'd never be able to figure it out. This place was cheap. In fact, they practically paid him to take it. So long as he took care of it and kept it up. And keeping it up didn't mean much. The place was run-down to start with.

High windows that swung open at the middle on hinges hung like droopy eyes. Spidered cracks in the glass were more common than not, and though this dirt road and parking lot saw a fair bit of traffic, from the outside it looked like not much worth caring about.

What Claude especially likes about this place is that it is out of the way. Down a dirt road that hardly anybody comes down anymore. And if they do, they obviously know they've been down the wrong road.

Still, some folks will come all the way into the parking lot and park their cars, seeing other cars here. Then they'll walk in through the slightly broken door and what they'll find inside is an old fat guy, Tyrell Murrell. He's probably smoking a cigarette and wearing clothes that would make you think he were a janitor or plumber or something.

And he'll look up at you lazily, like nothing's going on. And when your eyes have adjusted to the dim interior, you'll see just a floor of old farm equipment and parts. Most of it's rusting and most of it doesn't look like it's worth a hill of beans.

But you'll be curious and you'll ask Ty, because that's what it says on his embroidered shirt—"Ty." You'll ask him, "What is all this stuff?"

And he'll look back down at his paper, maybe take a pull on his smoke, and he'll say, "It's old farm equipment."

That's obvious, but really, that's all it is. And then you'll ask him about the directions and he'll be helpful, but in a really tired, bored-with-his-job kind of way. And you'll get on your way. Because if you don't, there are at least three snipers, probably five or six, who could blow your head open like a piñata before you even realized you'd been shot.

Claude smiles and gets out of his car. He looks at the decrepit building. The best government engineers spent a long time making this place look like it could just about fall down if you breathed too hard. Yet it's solid as a rock.

Claude walks in through the main door. It's a single metal door, and inside it's dark. Yellow lights hang from the ceiling, dribbling dim light about like they're flakes of real gold.

Ty looks up from his chair. He's a big African-American guy, stronger and faster than his heft would suggest. He's one of Claude's old friends from Langley, since retired, but he came back to work for NANA. Ty smiles, big and wide.

"Claude, good to see you, my man."

Claude smiles at him. "Tyrell, how you holding up?"

"Good, you know. This gig's too easy. Sometimes too boring, but I got my vices." He picks up the National Inquirer and assorted rags and flaps them about before putting them down.

"You know that stuff will rot your brain."

Tyrell laughs, loud, leaning back, and his guttural laugh is like a rhythmic base strum. "Ah, Claude, my thirty-five years in Langley already rotted it."

Claude smiles and walks up to the desk and shakes his hand. "Good to see you again, old friend," he says.

Tyrell nods. "They're waiting for you. Got some good toys for you, so I hear."

At the back of this warehouse, there's an old combine looking in rough shape. It's just the body. The wheels and the header aren't attached. It sits, solid on the concrete floor.

Like everything that Claude has any say over, all the parts in here are American made. Like this combine; it's a John Deere.

Claude climbs up into the cab. He faces backward in it. Behind the seat is a small metal box. He opens it and places his thumb on a reader. At eye height, a screen that couldn't be detected before slides open, and out comes a small metallic arm with what looks like an egg cup on the end. Claude places his right eye on it and a laser reads his retina.

"Black moon ugly maiden wheel square," he says.

Claude is a big believer in security and redundancy. Everybody who needs access to this facility—and there are close to a hundred of them—has to get in this way. Not necessarily through the combine; there are other avenues within this warehouse to access the R&D basement. But each requires fingerprints, retina identification, voice identification, coupled with a one-time secret passphrase that expires after three hours from creation.

The metal at the back of the cab, which Claude is in front of, opens up and he steps into the grain tank. This whole combine has been modified, but you wouldn't know it from the outside. You couldn't even tell from inside the cab unless you knew what you were looking for.

Inside the grain tank is a lift which slowly brings Claude 150 feet down into NANA's belly, though really, this is NANA's brain. This is where the magic happens.

Claude steps out of the elevator after the doors open into a large, brightly lit whitewashed room. A woman stands up and comes around from her desk. She is dressed in gray slacks and a blue blouse underneath a white overcoat. Her brown hair is back in a small ponytail.

"Hello, Claude, we have some very good news for you," she says.

Claude takes her offered hand and shakes it. "Thank you, Kathleen."

On the breast of her coat is embroidered "Dr. Kathleen L. Butler." Claude has no idea about what the L stands for; more than that, he finds it pretentious. But that's what you seem to get when you hire the brightest. Nobody who comes down here— well, except for Claude, Yolanda, and a few others—has less than a doctorate in their specific field.

The salaries for these engineers and scientists are huge. Even larger than what they would get in the private sector. But they're worth every penny. This is where the bulk of NANA's budget goes. To R&D, technology, and salaries required for that R&D.

Claude looks at Kathleen and smiles. She probably has no idea that she makes more than five times what he does. But he doesn't mind. These are the sacrifices required to make America safe. Kathleen is head of R&D for NANA.

One of the reasons Claude appointed her for the job is because she's discreet. She doesn't ask questions to which she won't like the answer. To her, ignorance is very much bliss when it comes to certain "problems" that she imagines Claude solves.

"Let's go into the briefing room," she says and leads Claude down the corridor, where they enter into a large room that has one-way windows looking out from where they came from and out toward a large closed-off area where scientists and engineers work in modified hazmat suits looking like white ghosts.

The hum of the electrical equipment is a pleasant background noise. NANA's brain is immaculate, not only out of necessity when working with such nanotechnology, but because Kathleen is a stickler for cleanliness.

Claude watches his engineers and scientists working with large equipment, lasers, computers, cutters, and other large manufacturing equipment. Such large and expensive equipment to make such small and deadly robots. Miniscule really. Claude realizes just how small they are. He's been told over and over again. These nanobots that everyone in here, except for him, have inside their brains and other areas of their body are a little larger than red blood cells and a little smaller than lymphocytes.

Kathleen heads on over to a desk and pushes the button on a microphone. "Dr. Daniel Chadbourne to the briefing room. Dr. Chadbourne to the briefing room, please."

She turns to look at Claude. "He's going to bring you the sample we've developed as per your request. And we've also got some really neat extra features that I think you'll like."

Claude beams. He pushes his large-framed glasses back onto the bridge of his nose. He feels like a kid on Christmas morning.

"This is going to make all the difference," he thinks.

Out of the corner of his eye, some movement catches his attention. He looks left, and way down the hall, from where he recently came, a short troll of a man is making his way toward the briefing room. He wobbles back and forth, walking toward them like a duck.

4:45 AM

Lisbon, Portugal

Maggie pushes the needle in deep enough to reach the heart. She empties the syringe and pulls the needle back out. She's been a doctor for a long time, but she's never been this scared over the outcome of a patient. Mostly that's because she really likes Tom. Actually, she thinks, maybe, just maybe, she might actually love him.

But it's more than that. There's nothing anyone could do for him right now, unless he were lying in the cardiac unit at Cleveland Clinic or perhaps the Mayo. But he's not, so everything about Tomo Daisen's life or death pivots on Maggie.

"What can we do?" asks James.

Maggie looks at him. Her eyes are starting to mist up. But that won't do. She blinks them away and swallows the hot knot of ragged lead in her throat.

"Start chest compressions," she says. "Other than that, there is nothing left for us to do. I've done all I can. We've done all we could. I just don't know why he didn't slip back into Alpha when I sent the nanos the message."

She puts the cap back on the needle and puts the syringe in a small biohazard box she has in her bag. Maggie's thinking about the reason the nanos might have ignored her messages. That's not supposed to happen. Under all the training, the years of training for the thousands of scenarios, that's never happened.

Across the bed, up on the wall is an analog clock. It's plain, not even trying to be fancy. James watches the clock's second hand tick by as he starts chest compressions. He's aiming for about two per second, but it seems slow. The second hand is stuck. It won't move; it hesitates then tumbles forward, like a drunk man moving and clinging between telephone poles.

"How long should this take to work?" asks Maurice.

Maggie looks at him, her face frowned and lined in worry. "It should be immediate."

She stops to think. She gave him the required amount, dammit, why isn't it working? She quickly looks into her bag and pulls out the vial. It has millimeter markings on it. She checks carefully. She did give him the exact amount. She can't give him any more or he'll die, that's for certain.

She looks over at Tom. James is working hard and fast. He's looking at the clock on the opposite side of the wall.

"Please, Tom, please, for me, come back," she thinks.

And then there's a gasp. Tom's mouth opens and he draws a big breath. She puts her hand instinctively on James's to stop him. He immediately stops the chest compressions and gets up off Tom. Another deep ragged breath.

"Turn him on his side in case there are any fluids in his lungs," she says.

Maurice pushes and James pulls Tom onto his side. Maggie can't remember the last time she was so excited by a man's breathing. She watches Tom breathe as if she were his lover, just awoken next to him as he sleeps. His breath starts to become more rhythmic. But it's fast, as it should be.

Maggie reaches around her neck and places the stethoscope's earpieces into her ears. She places the chest piece on Tom's chest and listens to his breathing. His lungs seem reasonably clear. That's a good sign. She listens to his heart. It's beating at about 150 to 160 beats per minute. Fast, to be sure, but that means he's alive and the Resusinate is working.

Tom's eye's flutter and open like butterfly wings. He looks at her, but his stare is vacant.

"Abbi...abbi," he says.

Maggie thinks he's saying "Maggie," but then realizes he isn't.

"You're here with us, Tom," she says in a soft, warm voice. "You're safe with us."

He opens his eyes wider and he tries to sit up.

"Just lie down and relax for a bit, Tom," Maggie says.

He doesn't have the strength anyway. So he does as he's told. Maggie reaches for a blood pressure monitor and puts it around his right bicep.

"I couldn't do it," Tom says.

Maggie is watching the monitor. Tom's blood pressure is high but not dangerous. She's content with the reading. She takes the cuff off his bicep and puts the equipment away.

"He was just a small boy," says Tom. "I couldn't do it."

"You couldn't do what?" asks Maggie.

"I couldn't kill him," he says.

"Bukhari?"

Tom nods.

"That's okay," she says. "We'll get him next time."

"Can you confirm there's not EOL on Bukhari, Maggie?" asks James.

"What, now?"

"Yes now."

Maggie gets up, miffed at the timing of this. Though, to be fair, Tom is out of danger by this point. James follows her to the table and sits down next to her. Maggie taps away at her laptop and connects to Bukhari's nanobot. James can read the signal; he doesn't need Maggie to tell him.

"No EOL," she says.

"Goddammit!" says James and he smacks the soft side of his fist down on the table. Maggie's laptop jumps as if scared.

Tom is getting up onto his elbows. He's leaning back against the headboard of the bed. His breathing is fast.

"I feel weird," he says, "like I'm on speed."

"That's the Resusinate," Maggie says from the table.

"The what?" Tom asks.

"I had to inject you with a drug to bring you back from the dead. We lost you for a minute or two," she says.

"What do you mean you lost me?"

"You went off rogue. We started getting hyperactive vitals and I tried calling you back through the nano, but you were unresponsive. I tried a nanon broadcast, none responded, so we had to physically bring you back. You died, Tom. You actually died."

Tom looks over at the clock. He feels especially alive now. More than alive, like he needs to get up and sprint a marathon. He doesn't like the rushed, vibrating feeling he's got inside, like his body is stuffed full of fire ants trying to eat their way out.

"Were you called by the white light?" asks Maurice with a big grin on his face.

Tom looks over at him somberly and shakes his head. "No, everything just went black, nothing."

"Ah ha, maybe you were on your way to hell then," says Maurice, playfully punching Tom on the shoulder.

Tom stares ahead at the clock. At the table, James is looking at Maggie's laptop. The signal from Bukhari is strong. It shouldn't be. It should be non-existent at this point after the nano sent EOL confirmation. James grits his teeth.

"We were ambushed by three men on camels with rifles," says Tom. He rubs his shoulder and looks down at it. It's sore but there's nothing wrong with it. "I got grazed by a bullet on my shoulder. They jumped over a sandbag wall I had created for protection. I managed to gut the one guy, but then my lights went out. I got smacked on the back of the head by a rifle butt I think."

Tom rubs the back of his head. He can't feel any goose egg, but his head is throbbing like he's been hit there, though he can't tell if that's the drug or vestigial memory.

"But you didn't eradicate the threat, did you?" asks James.

James is trying to remain cool. In all his many years of training, military training, secret ops, and leading troops, he never met anyone as multi-dimensionally capable as Tom. And here is Tom, making the biggest fuckup that James ever saw. If someone had told him this would happen, not only wouldn't he have believed it, he would have punched them in the mouth for spewing filth. Yet here is Tom. James's brightest star, tarnished.

Tom doesn't look at any of them. He's trying to deal with the fire ants eating him inside out. He's trying to get used to the idea that he was brought back from the dead, and he's also trying to understand what went wrong.

"No, I didn't, Jim," Tom says. "He was a boy, my son, a six-year-old."

"Goddammit, Tom, he's not a boy; he's not your son. He's a goddam general in a terrorist regime hell-bent on nuking the free world, and he's sleeping pretty somewhere here in Lisbon."

"Actually," corrects Maggie, "he's awake now. The dream jolted him awake."

"Shit," says James under his breath. "Now we've got an international catastrophe on our hands. What do you think's gonna happen when he realizes that two of his colleagues dropped dead in their hotel room with no signs of foul play? I could've gone in myself. Now, we'll have to wait until he falls asleep if he does again before he gets back to Iran."

"I don't know what happened. Have any other agents had to deal with killing children?" asks Tom.

"Yeah, it's happened before, Tom. These aren't children we're killing, despite how they might appear in their dreams," says James.

"I can't explain it. There was just this overwhelming emotional connection I had with the boy. It was almost overpowering. I tried to think about killing him, but I couldn't. I got the knife out of its sheath, but I just couldn't do it. There was such a huge sense of love and emotion I felt, it hampered my abilities."

"Maybe that's it!" says Maggie. "Maybe that's what severed the connection to us. Your emotional connection to the elements in the dream was so strong, it overrode the nanos. We've all been trained to remain unemotionally connected. Maybe that's the reason why, not just to make us more efficient, but to maintain connection."

"While you two are pontificating the smaller issues of why and how, we have a real loose cannon to deal with now. What if Bukhari starts trying to figure out what happened to his colleagues? If you know what you're looking for, these nanos can be found by most modern medical facilities."

"I'm sorry, James, okay. I really am," says Tom. "But who else has ever gone for a hat trick in one night, let alone in one hour?"

Tom looks at James, holding his gaze. James doesn't say anything. He breaks the stare and glances over at Maggie's laptop.

"I didn't think so," says Tom.

7:47 PM

Run-Down Industrial Plant, Outside Washington, D.C.

Dr. Daniel Chadbourne enters the briefing room. His hair is a mess of brown curls over a cherubic face. His complexion is ruddy, but not from drinking. In fact, Daniel doesn't touch the stuff. Not after he's seen what it did to his mother, a mean alcoholic. He has thick round black-rimmed glasses. Thinner rectangular ones would suit his face better. But he doesn't care, and Claude doesn't have much fashion sense either.

Daniel wears a white overcoat like Kathleen's with his name embroidered on the left chest pocket. "Daniel R. Chadbourne Ph.D." it says. Daniel's proud of his Ph.D., which he got from MIT in Theoretical Physics. He likes to tell people that. His thesis was on the possibility of FTL. He's convinced it's a workable theory if technology would just catch up with his brainpower, as he likes to call it.

Claude doesn't have a clue what the "R" stands for. But he starts to think about it. Robert, Roger, Richard, Rockford, Remington, Retard. A smile creeps over Claude's face as he looks at Daniel, thinking that perhaps the "R" is for Retard. Then he thinks maybe the "L" for Kathleen's middle name is Loser. He looks over at her and she's looking at Daniel. Claude brings himself back to the present. He's being childish and unkind. That's unpatriotic, he thinks.

"Mr. Martin, this is Dr. Daniel Chadbourne, our head of theoretical research," says Kathleen introducing them to each other.

"It's very nice to meet you, Mr. Martin," says Daniel, offering a limp hand.

Claude takes his hand and shakes it. It's soft and warm, like shaking a turd, Claude imagines. He winces a smile at Daniel.

"Hello, Dan."

"Daniel."

Only his mother called him Dan, and that was Danny when he was very young. Everyone else calls him Dr. Chadbourne except for very close friends and his employer who he's looking at right now. They can call him Daniel. Not Dan.

Claude doesn't say anything. He takes his hand off the warm turd and subconsciously wipes it against his pant leg. Kathleen notices the awkwardness. Daniel might not be the most socially astute at NANA, but he's one of the brightest. Perhaps the brightest they have. He's just not a...well, he's just not a people person.

"Dr. Chadbourne has developed the nanobots you requested. Additionally, he has invented a variety of other applications that none of us thought about until he mentioned it. In hindsight, it seems so silly that we overlooked it. Anyway, I'll let Dr. Chadbourne explain," says Kathleen.

Informally, and amongst his peers or the rest of the scientists and engineers at NANA, Dr. Chadbourne is Daniel to her, but she knows how much he likes to hear the doctor in front of his name, so she indulges him in front of others and especially in front of their boss, Claude. She knows he eats it up. She can't blame him, really. He's worked hard to get where he is and he's earned the respect he deserves.

"Please have a seat, Claude, so we can show you what we've done," says Kathleen.

The three of them take a seat at a white table with several chairs around it. They're sitting together. Daniel is in the middle and Claude is on Daniel's left and Kathleen is to his right. Daniel places his fingers on the table, which looks as smooth as white marble. The table comes to life. Lights, buttons, words, and a keyboard appear in the general area where Daniel's hands are.

Daniel taps away at the keyboard and soon a holographic screen appears, emanating from the middle of the table. It is large and crystal clear. It shows the image of a mannequin.

"As you know, our vectors can deliver the nanos from anywhere. So long as there is general contact with the host, they can deliver the nanos to the brain, or anywhere else we want them. So far, from what I understand, nanos have been used only in the brain," says Daniel.

The image in front of them shows an animated video of a mosquito landing on the mannequin.

"Now, historically what we've used as vectors are robotic organisms, like this robotic mosquito you see before you," Daniel continues.

The animated video continues and zooms in on the mosquito. The mosquito thrusts its proboscis into the neck of the mannequin. The video zooms in at a much higher magnification and shows a cutaway of the proboscis. Dozens of little nanobots, looking much like real robots, pour into the mannequin through the mosquito's proboscis.

Claude is a little bored. He's seen this animated video a few times. They haven't updated it in a few years, not that they should. That's not where the money should be spent on. Nevertheless, he'd like to get to the prize. Time is safety. Americans think time is money, but that is only because folks like Claude and his team make time safe. Without safe time, nobody can make money. That's the unwritten motto of NANA, tempus est salus.

"Using a vector that can actually inject a nano into the host is especially helpful. You see, these little robots have engines, obviously, in order to move around and such. These are little ATP engines, pretty much identical to the engines within each cell of our bodies."

A new animated video shows in front of them of a little turnstile that looks like it's made up of knotted string.

"This is sort of how an ATP engine works. It's very efficient," says Daniel. "We're hard-pressed to improve on Mother Nature, and another benefit of creating an ATP engine is that once the nano is inside the host, it can find fuel wherever it happens to be. The body is full of ATP, relatively speaking, so once the nano is inside it can theoretically 'live' forever."

"This is all fascinating, Daniel, but I'm not sure it's information I need to know," says Claude.

Daniel doesn't look at him. He readjusts his glasses farther up his nose and taps away at the keyboard.

"Bear with me, sir," says Daniel. "I'm getting to the important parts. Our nanos have the engine, but we don't have the fuel."

On the holographic image is a blown-up graphic of a nanobot. It reminds Claude of a toy robot he had once as a young boy. The image slowly twirls around, giving them a 360-degree view.

"You can see here that the nano is all technology. When you're working down at this small scale—remember, the nano is roughly the size of a blood cell—you don't have a lot of room for extraneous material. So, we don't have any space for fuel, but we need an engine to power our nano. That engine is an ATP engine which works extremely well and very efficiently once inside the host. But we've got to get it into the host. So we use a vector, like a mosquito, to inject them."

Another nano is projected in front of them on the holographic screen. It's a twin of the first, though it looks like an older brother. A little broader and a little taller.

"This is nano 2.0," says Daniel, smiling. "He looks the same, doesn't he?"

He looks over at Claude. Daniel is savoring this moment. This is his time to shine.

"It looks almost identical. A bit wider and taller perhaps," answers Claude.

Daniel nods. "Yes sir, you're correct. These images are to scale. Nano 2.0 is slightly bigger, which helps stuff it with more technology, but that's not the real coup. Take a closer look."

The images rotate side by side. On the back of nano 2.0 is what appears to be a backpack.

"Looks like he's wearing a backpack of some sort," says Claude.

He's not impressed. Backpacks don't impress him. They're usually filled with junk that most people don't need to be carrying around.

"Bingo," says Daniel. "But this is not an ordinary backpack. This is a backpack filled with ATP. It is our fuel for the ATP engine. Now, the human body has this remarkable ability to recycle ATP almost ad infinitum. We haven't managed to do that with our nano's ATP engines. So, this ATP fuel cell on nano 2.0's back is like a battery. It will eventually run down."

Claude nods, feigning interest. He's not sure this is a breakthrough worthy of the hundreds of millions of dollars this facility burns through each year.

"I'm still not getting it," he says, leaning back in his chair, arms folded in front of him.

6:42 AM

Lisbon, Portugal

Armin has been awake for almost two hours. He woke up with a shiver from a bad dream. He was a boy with his family in the desert, but there was something odd about the man who was supposed to be his father. Armin can't pinpoint what it is. He knows that dreams are strange at the best of times, but this man, this image of his father, had a reality to it that seemed almost palpable. And he wasn't an Iranian. He wasn't his father. Armin felt a malevolence from him. The way he held the Janbiya. It was like he wanted to use it on Armin.

Armin did his Fajr prayers at around five thirty. It helped ease his troubled mind. He came out of the bath not long ago and the troubles started to renew themselves. Chewing at his mind like a dog might a rubber ball.

Armin decides to visit his colleagues. He didn't bother calling them to Fajr prayers. Neither man was as devout as he was, and neither of them gave any indication of wanting to join him in morning prayers either. Armin doubted they even took part in morning prayers regularly.

He called Farzan and Milad but neither of them answered. He wasn't surprised by Farzan. The boozer was likely still in an alcoholic stupor. But Milad, surely Milad would have answered. There was a chance he had gone out to order coffee and have an early pastry, but surely he would have passed Armin's door and realized Armin was up.

They had been given three suites right next to each other. Armin's is the closest to the elevator bank. As you exited Armin's suite, Milad's is next on the right, and Farzan's beyond his.

Armin knocks quietly on Milad's door. There is no answer. He peers into the peephole, but that's not how it's meant to work. It's a black splotch of ink. Armin knocks a little louder. Still no answer.

"Milad," he says quietly.

Nothing.

"Dr. Milad, it's Armin," he says more loudly.

Surely Milad must be able to hear him by now. Armin knocks still harder. No response. He moves over to Farzan's door and does the same thing.

"General Farzan Najafi, it's General Bukhari," he says.

His voice is bold and resonates with authority. This is not a good sign. Armin walks back to his room and picks up the phone and dials the operator.

"I need security," he says. "I need you to open up the rooms to my colleagues, General Najafi and Doctor Saatchi. Rooms 709 and 711."

"Very good, sir. Security will be up shortly. Can I tell them what is wrong?"

"I don't know, but I have phoned and knocked and called out and they don't answer. This is very unlike them."

"We'll be right up, sir."

The voice is well polished, the English impeccable. This is what you get from five-star hotels the world over. Armin hangs up the receiver and picks it up again. He calls the Iranian Embassy.

"Put me through to the Ambassador. Tell him it's General Armin Bukhari."

After a courteous exchange, Armin is put on hold. He doesn't have to wait long.

"Ambassador Nader."

"Ambassador, it's General Armin Bukhari, I need you at the Tiara Park Atlantic Lisboa Hotel. I have a bad feeling about what has happened to General Najafi and Doctor Saatchi."

"What do you mean?"

"We don't have time, Ambassador. I need to call Tehran, and hotel security is on their way up. We're in rooms 707 through 711."

"I'll be right there."

Armin gets up from his bed and takes a peak outside his room. No sign of security yet. He goes back to his bed and dials a number to Tehran.

"Hello."

"Doctor Usama Handal, please."

"Speaking."

"Usama, it's General Armin Bukhari."

"Armin, hello, how is your trip?"

"Not good, Usama, not good. I don't have long so please listen carefully. I think Farzan and Milad might have been assassinated. I don't know how, but they might have tried to kill me while I slept too."

"How can that be? How do you know?"

"I don't know, not for certain. I've just got a bad feeling. Our Canadian businessman we were supposed to meet the other day died in his sleep the night before our final meeting to sign the contract. Apparently it was heart failure. The contract is now on hold until BattleBuilt reorganizes. Anyway, I think the same might have happened to Farzan and Milad."

"What can I do?"

"What I need you to do is to think about how someone could be assassinated in their sleep. Put your best minds to it."

Outside his room, Armin hears the elevator doors open and two men in suits walk by his room. They then return and wait outside his open door.

"I've gotta go. I'm about to find out if this has truly happened. I'll be in touch."

Armin puts the phone down and walks to the door to greet the hotel security officers. Armin shakes their hands.

"I'm Affonso Barca, chief of security, and this is my right-hand man, Dinis Estacio."

Armin follows them to Milad's suite. Affonso knocks loudly. Three knocks. He pauses and does it again. Another pause and three loud knocks.

"Dr. Saatchi, this is hotel security. Can you please open up?"

Affonso's voice is baritone, loud like a big drum. He's probably woken up the whole floor by now. At least those who are still sleeping. They wait for what seems like an hour, though it is less than a minute. Affonso nods at Dinis who uses his card reader to unlock the door. It unlocks both locks. Dinis opens the door but it is stopped by the latch from the inside.

Dinis steps back and Affonso cranes his neck to see in as much as he can. He can't see much more than a sliver of the room, and his view doesn't give him a line of the bed.

"Dr. Saatchi," Affonso says, "this is hotel security. Can we come in? Are you okay, sir?"

Armin stands behind the two men, his hands clasped in front of him. He appreciates their thoughtfulness, though he'd rather they just get on with it.

Affonso steps back and again nods to Dinis. Dinis is a big man. Armin would judge him at about 6 feet 5 and 250 pounds, and none of it would be fat. Dinis puts his left shoulder close to the open side of the door. He takes a slight step back on his right leg and then slams up against the door like an iron statue. The latch gives as if it were made of toothpicks and it pulls a sliver of door frame with it.

The door swings open wide. Affonso and Dinis walk in, followed by Armin. They do a sweep of the room, heading into the bathroom and then back out, looking for anyone who shouldn't be in here. Armin is certain that only Milad is inside.

Armin walks in and toward the bed. Milad is tucked in. It looks like he is peacefully asleep. Though Armin knows better. Being a career soldier, he knows what death looks like. He knows the early stench of it too. His friend is dead. He places his finger on Milad's neck to be certain. No pulse.

Armin reaches up to the covers tucked under Milad's neck and pulls them down and off the bed. Milad is in his blue pajamas. Long pants and long-sleeved top. There is no indication at all of any foul play.

"I need to call the police, sir," says Affonso.

Armin nods. "Let us first check on General Najafi," he says.

8:00 PM

Run-Down Industrial Plant, Outside Washington, D.C.

Backpacks are usually used by travelers and hikers. Claude isn't paying millions of dollars a year to let a bunch of small robots go hiking around the countryside. Claude looks over at Daniel. "A very odd little man," he thinks.

"Why have you given these robots backpacks? Are they tourists now?" Claude is still leaning back in his chair, arms folded. He's not impressed. Well, at least he's not very impressed. He has been delighted with what they've managed to create so far. These nanobots are outstanding, but adding a backpack is not something he thinks is groundbreaking work.

"I know what you're thinking," says Daniel, not looking at Claude. "But this backpack is an incredible feat of technological breakthrough on the small scale."

Nano 1.0 and nano 2.0 keep spinning around in front of them, very slowly.

Daniel continues, "Let me see if I can't explain it to you in layman's terms to help get the point across."

Claude raises an eyebrow, not sure if he's detected sarcasm. "I beg your pardon," he says.

"Sorry, sir, I meant no disrespect. I just want you to fully appreciated the breakthrough we have before us." Daniel is fidgeting, his face becoming a little flushed.

"Carry on then, Daniel."

"What we've managed to do with nano 2.0 with this backpack is vastly improve how we can deliver the nanos to the host target. With this little backpack, the nano is now capable of self-power for a little over an hour."

Claude thinks he's starting to get it. "So we no longer have to inject the nano into the host in order to deliver them?"

Daniel looks over at Claude and beams. "Exactly," he says. "This is the benefit of it."

Claude nods. This is a big breakthrough. Injecting nanos always left a trace, or at the very least a memory. Not many people get bitten by a mosquito without knowing it. Claude has always been weary of the vectors they've used to deliver the nanos. After all, with some ingenuity and creativity, if someone ends up not getting assassinated and remembers being bitten— well, you could slowly put two and two together.

Now that you can deliver the nano without having to inject it, the host will arguably never know. Claude looks at Kathleen.

"And without injecting the nanos, the host should not feel them enter him at all. Correct?"

Kathleen is all smiles. She knows how big this breakthrough is. "Precisely. I'll let Dr. Chadbourne continue."

"Only the most sensitive of hosts, people, would feel anything," Daniel says. "And if they did feel anything, it might feel like a slight tickle or an itch."

"Have you tried this on anyone yet?" asks Claude.

"We haven't gotten to that stage yet, but that's next. Now to put this in perspective, what would an hour's worth of fuel offer us as far as distance traveled? These nanobots can move at the human-adjusted size equivalent of about sixty miles an hour."

"That seems pretty fast," says Claude. He's beginning to feel enthusiastic again about the technology. His mind is spinning thinking about all the possibilities.

"Yes, it is. Speed was one of the criteria that we needed for the type of work we do. However, once inside the body, the nano can travel quite quickly along the body's own highways, the arteries and other blood vessels. But once out, it needs to move on its own steam."

"So, at what maximum distance can we deliver these robots in order to ensure they end up in the host?"

"Well, sir, these nanos have the ability to power themselves for about an hour at the human-sized equivalent of sixty miles an hour. Therefore, if they were human-sized, or about six feet, they could travel sixty miles. But they're not. At their very, very small size, the distance they can travel on their own steam is almost two inches."

Claude looked down at his thumb. His whole thumb was about two inches. That didn't seem very much distance at all. He was starting to feel the pang of disappointment.

"For best results," Daniel continues, "we suggest applying the nanos to the host in order to ensure that they can bury in from outer clothing."

"Help me understand this in practical terms, as I'm starting to feel less impressed than I was earlier."

Daniel's steam is starting to lag. This is huge and Claude doesn't appreciate it. "That's the problem with plebians," he thought. "They don't appreciate brainpower."

"Well, we're working on increasing the fuel cell's power," says Kathleen, "but something to bear in mind, Claude, is that when you're talking about something this small, you have to appreciate the ability of size and scale. What I mean by this is that with the nano being so small, what would be considered fast at our scale, that is, sixty miles per hour, only breaks down to two inches per hour at the nano scale."

Claude looks at her and nods.

"If these nanos at their size could even manage to keep up with us at walking speed, which is about 3 miles per hour, they would be traveling at a human-sized equivalent speed of roughly 300,000 miles per hour. These nanos are about 100,000 times smaller than we are."

"I see," says Claude, and he does see; he is beginning to understand.

"I would never say never, but getting these nanos up to that kind of speed is a herculean task. Furthermore, I'm not sure it's practical. There are several problems involved with leaving something so small unattached to anything. For example, if we had some nanos sitting here on the table, just the air currents, which we can't detect, would be buffeting them around as if they were in a hurricane."

"Right, I understand."

"But think of the applications already available to us now that we no longer have to inject the nanos."

Kathleen holds out her hand. "Pleased to meet you," she says, shaking the air. "Tag—you're it. Just by touch, we have the ability to deliver nanos, and this is pure stealth. No longer are hosts getting injected, which as you can well imagine leaves us somewhat vulnerable to being discovered at some point. Now, no one will be the wiser that they've been infected."

A light bulb comes on in Claude's mind. This is how he will deliver the goods to the president during their next meeting. He smiles broadly.

"Excellent, excellent. I like it."

Daniel pulls out a small white cylinder. It's about the size of a lip balm. He offers it to Claude. Claude accepts it and looks at it.

"This is your nano delivery system," he says, "as you requested. It looks like a lip balm and acts very similarly. You take the cap off, but instead of smearing it on your lips, you smear it on your fingers or palm. It will dry and become undetectable within a few minutes, but the nanos are still clinging to your palm. If you wipe your palm against anything or you shake hands, hundreds of nanos will transfer to whatever it is you've touched or whoever you've shaken hands with."

"Good work. But what's to prevent the nanos to just start burying into me?"

"They're not activated until you activate them, at which time they'll go to work. This particular batch we've given you, sir, can only be activated by your own personal code and passphrase. They're coded to you." Daniel enjoys the cloak and dagger stuff as much as the next nerd.

"Excellent, but if I activate them, I'll likely still have some left on me, correct?"

Daniel nods. "Correct."

Daniel reaches into his lab coat and pulls out a black rectangle. It looks like a slim digital camera. He hands it to Claude.

"This is an EMP camera," he says. "I won't show you how it works, but it works exactly like it looks like it should work. Use it like a point-and-shoot camera. It has a broad scattering but short length pulse. So long as you point it at yourself and you do so within six feet, it will destroy any electrical device within an eight feet bubble. This includes the nanos, so you'll want to make sure when you are cleaning yourself with this EMP that the nano balm I just gave you is in another room along with any other electronics that you wish to protect."

Claude is grinning like the kid he was when he got his first bike from Santa when he was six years old. "Genius," he says. "So this has an effective range of around eight feet?"

"Yes, if you look at the lens of that EMP camera and imagine a bubble coming out of it that has a diameter of eight feet, anything within that bubble will be fried. And it's harmless to humans and other living organisms."

"Good, very well done, Daniel, Kathleen." Claude looks at them both and smiles broadly like a proud father.

"There is something else we'd like to show you," says Kathleen. "Thanks for joining us Daniel."

"You're welcome," he says.

Daniel gets up and leaves the briefing room. Kathleen starts tapping away at the keyboard that has now appeared under her hands which rest on the table in front of them.

"These new nanos," Kathleen says, "are capable of attaching themselves anywhere in the body we'd like them to. As such, they can be used to monitor heart rate, respiration, or anything else. We've been using them as, and focused on them as being, agents of assassination. They send an electrical impulse to the heart that shuts it down. But there is so much more we can do."

"I'm intrigued."

"Take a look at this," she says, tapping away at the keyboard.

On the holographic screen in front of them, what looks like a video appears. There is no sound. The video looks like a first-person account of somebody running through narrow city streets in the day. Up ahead, a man looks over his shoulder. He's scared; there is fear written all over his face. The runner is catching up to him. Kathleen freezes the image.

"Interesting. What is that?"

"That's our Agent Algernon Sorel, streaming live from Jakarta."

Claude is not that impressed. "So, he's wearing some sort of steadycam. Big deal."

"Take another look."

The video restarts. The runner, Agent Sorel, is ducking down a narrow street. It's dark being in the shadows as the buildings block out the light; his prey is almost at the end of this street. Nobody else is around. It's eerily quiet and there is no sound, just visuals. Agent Sorel stops and you see his hands come up, holding a handgun. He fires. His hands jerk up and back down again. The man he was running after falls to the ground. Agent Sorel starts off running toward him again. Kathleen freezes the image.

"Do you notice anything special about this video?"

"Not in particular. The quality is great; there's almost no shake for a steadycam, but why is this being recorded without my authorization?" There is a little bit of tension in Claude's voice. He runs a tight ship, and somebody's going to pay for recording without his authority.

"Nothing's being recorded," says Kathleen. "This is live streaming from Agent Sorel's optic nerve. We have placed a nano there and it is reading, decoding, and sending the signals direct to us as it happens. Basically, we are seeing what Sorel is seeing."

"Does he know?"

"No, but we could tell him if you want."

Claude shakes his head. He likes it better this way. This opens up a whole new window of opportunities, verifications, and control.

"What about audio? Can we only get visual?"

Kathleen taps at the keyboard again. The video continues. Agent Sorel is now looking at the dead man. He's leaning over him. You can hear Sorel's ragged breath. He leans down to check on the man's pulse at his neck. In the background you can hear police sirens.

"Vacate, Sorel. We can get him another day," says Sorel's handler.

"Target has been eradicated," says Sorel.

Kathleen pauses the transmission and looks at Claude.

"Pretty much anything is now available to us. What the agents can see and hear, we can see and hear."

Claude looks at her. She is worth her weight in gold. This is why he hires only the best. But he has one question.

"Is this technology backward compatible? Can we make use of it in the nanos already engaged?"

Kathleen smiles. "Is America the best country in the world?" she asks rhetorically.

7:08 AM

Lisbon, Portugal

Affonso is not willing to wait quite as long at General Najafi's door as he did at Doctor Saatchi's. He raps on the outside door, once and then twice. The raps are firm and echo down the hall.

"General Najafi, hotel security. Can you open the door please?"

Affonso waits for about a count of thirty. Then he looks over at Dinis and nods. Dinis puts his security card into the door and it opens up both locks. Dinis opens up the door tenderly, expecting it to catch on the latch. It does. He looks at Affonso.

Affonso nods his head, more frustrated this time. "Open it," he says quietly.

Armin is standing behind the two hulking men. He moves back to the far side of the hallway as a maid trundles by with her housekeeping trolley. Armin smiles at her and she returns it.

Dinis puts his shoulder to the door. This is the second one he's ever broken down in his career. The first one was just a few minutes ago. He has a feel for it. He hammers his bodyweight against the door more gently, giving it just enough to break it open. The door does so and they walk in.

The two security officers disappear into the bathroom while Armin goes straight toward the bed. Unlike Milad, Farzan looks dead. He is on his right side facing the curtain, and his left hand is out of the blankets and hanging over the edge of the bed. Blood has pulled into this hand. It looks like a purple puffer fish. Farzan's black hairs are like spikes, all standing straight up as if his hand were a pincushion stuck full of black pins.

Armin takes the general's pulse, but there's nothing there. Even his head is lolling at an awkward angle, and his pallor is an ashen gray. Armin finds no pulse, and he pulls the sheets down from over the general. The general is in his navy blue silk pajamas. Long sleeves, the left of which is bunched up around his bicep. Long pants too. There is no indication of violence or foul play.

"Just like how they said they'd found Amaury," thinks Armin.

Affonso is on the phone with the police. He hangs up and comes and stands next to Armin.

"I'm terribly sorry about this, General. The police are on their way."

"It is suspicious," says Armin.

Affonso looks at him with a small frown. "No signs of foul play, General."

"I know. That's the secret."

Affonso doesn't understand what the General is talking about. He looks over at Dinis. "Go secure the other room until the police get here. Keep the door mostly closed for privacy."

Dinis nods and leaves Farzan's room, closing the door behind him. Moments later there is a knock at the door. Affonso goes to answer it. He comes back in with three men. Armin knows the shorter and older of the three men.

"Doctor Nader," says Armin, shaking the man's hand.

"General, so good to see you again, but not under these circumstances."

Armin nods and they walk back to the foot of the bed where Nusrah looks at Farzan.

"Inna lillahi wa inna ilayhi raji'un," says Nusrah.

"Verily we belong to God, and to God we return," repeats Armin.

"I was on the phone with Usama on the way here," says Nusrah, "and he tells me you suspect"—he pauses and lowers his voice—"assassination?"

Armin nods. "I do."

"And yet, I see no evidence of foul play, Armin."

"I know. That is their genius."

"Then how?"

"I don't know. But when the coroner comes, I want him to determine time of death." Armin looks at his watch. "I will tell you now, that if I am right, Farzan and Milad were murdered at around 4:30 to 4:45 AM."

Nusrah looks at Armin with incredulity. "Why this time?"

"It was at around 4:45 that I woke up from a strange and terrible dream. I dreamed that my father was thinking of killing me with his Janbiya, only he wasn't my father; somehow, I had a bad feeling about him. Something wasn't quite right. But before he could kill me—I was a boy of six in the dream—we were attacked by men on horses. I know it seems strange, but this was unlike any dream I have ever had. It was more real, more sinister, much more foreboding."

"If you are right, what does it mean?"

Armin looks at Nusrah and puts his hand on his shoulder. "My old friend, if I am right, then it means the Americans have found new ways of killing us. More discreet ways. What that is, I have no idea. Therefore, we must get Farzan and Milad to Doctor Handal and his colleagues for a thorough autopsy. Make sure that the Portuguese understand that. Time is of the essence."

There is another knock at the door which Affonso answers. Armin hears a lot of Portuguese being spoken, and when the men enter the main bedroom, he knows they are police by their uniform. There is also an older man, think, with a handlebar moustache in a white overcoat carrying what looks like a doctor's bag.

A tall man, the oldest of three police officers, comes up to Nusrah and shakes his hand.

"I am Inspector Mateus Lagos of the Judicial Police."

"Inspector, I am Ambassador Nusrah Nader of the Islamic Republic of Iran, and this is my colleague General Armin Bukhari."

Inspector Lagos nods at Armin. "You called security to check on"—Lagos takes out a notebook from his chest pocket and flips a few pages—"General Najafi and Doctor Saatchi?"

Armin nods. "I did."

"It says here that you suspected foul play?"

"I just had a feeling. As you can see, Inspector, there is no foul play. Sadly, it appears that my colleagues died naturally."

"Yes, but Doctor Saatchi is a man in his mid-forties, no?"

Nusrah nods. "That is true, Inspector, and we are sorry to have troubled you, but even men in their forties can die of heart attacks. I will have his doctor send over medical documentation. Doctor Saatchi was not in the best of health. He had a weak heart from rheumatic fever he caught as a young boy."

Lies, or rather, political maneuverings come easily to Nusrah, especially when the Islamic Republic of Iran's interests were in jeopardy. He doesn't want to make this any harder than it needs to be. If he can just get the police out, the coroner will be easy.

"I will take a look around and make my own determination if you don't mind, Ambassador."

Nusrah smiles at the Inspector. "I am not here to get in your way, Inspector."

The coroner comes forward and holds out a bony hand to Nusrah. His gray handlebar moustache gives him an air of aristocracy to what is otherwise a gaunt, skeletal appearance. His head is covered with wisps of gray-white hair that makes him look like he just took his head out of a cotton candy machine.

"I am Doctor Reinaldo Monterroso. I am the coroner on duty. Would you allow me to examine the body?"

"Yes, though we wish to have both General Najafi and Doctor Saatchi brought back to Iran as soon as possible. We will conduct the autopsy there," says Nader.

"I understand."

Reinaldo heads over to Farzan's corpse and pulls out his tools and starts to examine the body. A few minutes later, Inspector Lagos comes back and watches Reinaldo. Reinaldo looks up at them after a time.

"It looks like death was from natural causes, but the actual cause can't be determined without an autopsy, which Ambassador Nader says will be done in Iran."

"Well," says Lagos, "I have found no evidence to contradict the coroner, so I am ruling this as a natural death. Is that agreeable to you, Ambassador?"

"It is, as we said."

"Very well. I will be off now with my men. As always, the Judicial Police is at your disposal, Ambassador, if you have any questions or require any further help."

Lagos shakes hands with Nader.

"As mentioned," Nader says, "we would like to get the bodies home to Iran for burial preparation as soon as possible. If you can help us with that, it would be greatly appreciated."

Lagos nods, shakes hands with Armin, and walks out the hotel suite with his two men behind him.

Nader turns to the coroner. "Can you give an approximate time of death, Doctor?"

Doctor Monterosso stands up and looks at Nader and then Bukhari. "Rigor mortis has not yet set in, the eyes are still clear, and with the temperature of the body at the moment, I would suggest that death was about three hours ago. Give or take a half hour."

Nusrah and Armin look at their watches. It is just a little past seven thirty.

"Thank you, Doctor," says Nusrah.

"I will go and check on Doctor Saatchi," says Monterosso as he leaves the two men still standing at the foot of the bed.

"You were right," says Nusrah, looking at Armin. "This is of utmost importance. I will be calling the president and the supreme leader as soon as I can. We must get to the bottom of this."

11:11 AM

A Professional Building, Washington D.C.

Claude looks at the lip balm container full of nanobots that stands upright in front of him on his desk. Proud like a soldier. Indeed, they are his good little soldiers. Claude has a meeting with the President lined up at 3 PM. He'll get there early; he is punctual and he takes pride in that. It won't matter today if the president keeps him waiting a half hour, an hour, hell, Claude won't care if the president keeps him waiting the whole day. Because today will be the last day he'll wait for a tardy, unpatriotic American, even if he is the POTUS.

Claude picks up the lip balm and puts it on its side and he rolls it across his desk calendar as if here were lovingly rolling a Cuban cigar. He never enjoyed a Cuban cigar, but they are by all accounts the best. In fact, Claude rarely smokes cigars, but he appreciates the fine art developed over the centuries in making them.

Claude brings the cylinder to his nose and inhales as he swipes the lip balm along his upper lip. He smells an odd combination of engine grease and vanilla. Claude takes the white lid off the top of the cylinder and looks at the balm inside. It is an unremarkable gray. He lightly rubs his thumb over it. It is wet and slightly tacky. He rubs the medicament between thumb and forefinger and within seconds the wetness has evaporated and the tackiness is undetectable.

Claude grins from ear to ear. "This will work just as planned," he thinks. There is a knock at his door. He opens the desk drawer in front of him and puts the lip balm there, amongst white paper, his 1911 R1 Carry, and a tin of mints—the curiously strong kind.

"Come in," he says.

Yolanda peeks her head around the corner of the door. Her face is serious. She carries no smile like she usually does.

"Do you have a minute, Claude?"

Claude nods. "I do. Come on in."

Yolanda comes in, closes the door behind her, and sits down in the chair across from him. Claude looks at her for a moment. She doesn't look happy, not that she's showing obvious signs, but Claude can read people. In a different life he might have been a professional poker player.

"I have some, um, unfortunate news."

"I figured."

Claude looks at her with a steady gaze. She's trying to soften the blow. He's not sure why she's doing that, he prefers brutal unclothed honesty above beating around the bush.

"Tell it to me straight, Yola," he says. "You know I like it better that way."

She nods and looks down at her lap. She takes a deep breath and steals some courage before looking up and holding Claude's gaze.

"Alpha Team messed up," she says, biting her lip and holding her breath.

Yolanda is not sure where to go from here. This has never happened before in NANA's history. Never before has a team botched an assassination. But then again, never has one agent been tasked with three kills in one night. In hindsight, that might have been asking too much, but Seaton swore that Daisen was up for it. He said it'd be on him if anything went wrong.

"Alpha Team is the Alpha for a reason. They're the best. What happened?" Claude's voice is calm. He's thinking, trying to understand what's going on. This is not going to be good news to have to tell the president. But he might not have to tell him. Claude steels himself. He's not going to let himself go like he did after the last meeting with the president.

"They left a target mobile."

"There was no erasure?"

"No, Claude, they left a man in the middle, a target now rogue and still very much alive."

"Tell me again what Alpha Team was doing?"

Yolanda shifts in her seat. She pauses and takes a moment to collect her thoughts. To think how best to summarize Alpha Team's mission.

"Alpha was tasked with the Iranian Intervention. It started with the Canadian businessman, Amaury Querry of BattleBuilt, who was going to provide them with nuclear technology and other weapons. The three Iranians were highly ranked officials inside of Iran's upper political echelon. General Farzan Najafi, the scientist Doctor Milad Saatchi, and General Armin Bukhari."

Claude does not take his eyes off Yolanda. There's a calmness in them as if he were off daydreaming. But he's listening to her every word, absorbing it all, sifting through it to uncover the best solution.

"Alpha Team has been in Lisbon on this mission," Yolanda continues. "We've recalled them back this morning. They should be arriving back any minute. Everything in Lisbon went well until the final assassination attempt, which, as chance would have it, was on General Bukhari. NINJA Tomo Daisen was unable to complete this last task."

Yolanda takes a moment to think about trying to apologize on his behalf. She looks at Claude. He grits his teeth but he doesn't say anything.

Yolanda goes on, "NINJA Daisen almost lost his life. They had to intervene with drugs to get him out of dreamscape. In fact, he was actually lost for a short while."

"Daisen is our best NINJA."

"Yes, Claude, he is."

"So what went wrong?"

"We're not sure yet. I haven't been able to debrief them fully, but it appears on his third Theta attempt, something happened in the dreamscape that prevented him being able to conclude the task at hand."

Claude rubs his chin with his forefingers and thumb. He doesn't like the sound of this. "You're telling me that Daisen had more than one Theta attempt that night?"

"Yes. It was his third that was unsuccessful."

"Dammit, Yola. We've modeled this; we've practiced it. There is great Theta and nano communication degradation after the first. We know this. What the hell were you thinking?"

"Yes, I know. I'm sorry, Claude. Seaton swore to me it could be done. He wanted to show you how good Daisen and the whole of Alpha was at this. He said it would be on him if anything went wrong."

"It will be on him."

Claude goes silent for a moment. Yolanda averts her gaze and looks down at her lap. She fiddles with her hands for a while. She feels terrible, like she let her own father down.

"I'm sorry, Claude," she says, her eyes wet with tears. "I really believed him. I really thought Alpha Team could pull this off. I know you've been under so much pressure lately, and with the president axing our budget, I thought this could be a way for us to remain incredibly relevant and useful. Doing more with less."

Claude gets up from his desk and walks around and stands behind her. He puts his hand on her shoulder and squeezes it gently. NANA is already stripped to the bone. He knows she was just doing her best. That's why she is his number one.

"I forgive you," he says. "This will be on Seaton. And Daisen. The whole of Alpha Team, actually. They should have known better. Seaton above all others."

Yolanda takes a tissue from her pocket and dabs at her eyes. "What will you do?"

Claude is looking at the painting of Watson and the Shark. Suddenly, he has a flash of inspiration. He grins and his mouth resembles that of the sharks.

"We will sacrifice the shark," he says.

2:50 PM

Oval Office, The White House

Claude can't help himself. He is always punctual. His father beat it into him. It is almost like a religion. "If you have no respect for yourself or God," he remembers his father saying, "then you can come and go as you please. But we have self-respect and more importantly respect for God."

Yolanda is not with him today. He'll make up some excuse if the president inquires, but he doubts the president will even care. Claude wants to keep Yolanda away from this as much as possible. She's his right hand, confidant, but more than that, she believes in keeping America safe just as he does. But he doesn't need her here for this part. In fact, for this part, he relishes the idea of being alone.

Claude has taken great care to keep the cylinder of nanobots safe. He gets out of his Taurus and closes the door. He can feel the cylinder in his right pocket amongst his loose change.

Claude walks up to the White House, his strides buoyant and long. He carries in his left hand a briefcase that contains just a few papers. He doesn't imagine he'll be sharing much of what's inside them with the president. He imagines this meeting will be just like the rest, the only difference being that it will determine the president's fate.

Claude carries a slight grin on his face that he just can't get off. He feels ebullient and righteous and unbeatable. At the main entrance he has to show both ID and a visitor's tag to a well-dressed security officer. He is also searched and has the contents of his pockets and briefcase investigated. He has already done this entering the gates, but he does not mind.

He walks down the hallways and at the door to the president's secretary's office he is met with two more secret service men. They too request ID and the visitor's tag. Unlike in the movies, they look at it carefully and scan the tag to verify it. They also do a thorough search, emptying his pockets onto a side table, and pat him down. They open the cap of the lip balm, the cylinder of which Claude has wrapped in a Blistex label. They take a thorough look at his briefcase and its contents. This is why he doesn't bring top secret documents; they're none of these men's business. They nod and the one man opens the door for him.

The secretary like an old librarian from a public school looks up at him over her glasses like he might have spoken too loud, yet he hasn't said anything. He walks up to her and presents his ID again.

"Claude Martin," he says, "for the President."

"I remember you from last time," she says, handing him back his ID.

Claude realizes that he needs to apply the nanos to his hand.

"Can you point me to the washroom?" he asks with his best smile.

The secretary is not smiling. He doesn't think she knows how. She's looking down at the papers at her desk. "Out the door and on your left, three doors down." Then she looks up at him. "You'll be searched again when you come back in."

"I don't mind," he says. "It's the only human touch I've been getting lately."

She doesn't see the humor in it, so Claude leaves. He heads out and finds the washroom easily. It is a small, single occupant washroom. He takes a moment to look around. He can't seem to find any cameras, though you never know. He hopes that the White House hasn't been riddled with CCTV. There is something to be said for a bit of privacy in a democracy. At least in a washroom.

Nevertheless, Claude is not certain, so he'll be putting on a show just in case he is being watched. He pulls his pants down and sits on the toilet and places his briefcase on this lap. He reaches into his pant's pocket and pulls out the lip balm of nanos. He opens the briefcase and keeping it at a forty-five degree angle he places his hands into its gaping mouth and applies the nanos to his right palm.

Claude groans and pretends to strain for a bit before deciding that he has accomplished his task. He uses some toilet paper to make sure the whole ruse looks authentic, though he uses his left hand which is not the hand he would usually use.

By the time he gets up from the toilet, his hand is already dry and you can't tell he's applied anything to it. He leaves the washroom without washing his hands; he doesn't want to sacrifice any nanos to the drain. After another search and pat-down, he reenters the secretary's office. She doesn't even look up, pecking away at her keyboard like her hands are starved chickens.

Claude is the only other person in here. He checks his watch. It's 3:00 on the nose. He wonders how long he'll have to wait for the tardy president. The last time he saw him, the president made him wait for seventeen minutes. Now that they've already met, Claude suspects he'll be waiting longer this time. He's not disappointed.

At 3:33 PM the president enters the secretary's office from the hallway, trailed by two secret service men. Claude stands up.

"Mr. President," he says, moving forward, but he's blocked by one of the men. He sits back down. President Towles nods at his secretary and she follows him into the Oval Office. They close the door behind them and leave the two secret service men standing outside. Claude looks at them. They're like statues, looking straight ahead at the door they just came in from.

Claude's pissed. "Patience," he thinks to himself, "is a virtue, and virtue is a grace and Grace is a lady with a very pretty face." It doesn't help. Then he reminds himself that this will be the last meeting he'll be having with the president. After this he'll be meeting with the vice president. A much better solution. He grits his teeth.

At 3:47 PM, the secretary comes out of the Oval Office.

"Mr. Martin, the president will see you now."

She lets him pass her and then closes the door behind him. Claude reaches out his right hand to shake the president's.

"Mr. President, thank you for seeing me again," he says, feigning a smile that glints wolf's teeth.

The president waves him away without shaking his hand.

"Shit," he thinks, "this is going to be harder than I thought."

"As you can imagine, Claude, I'm very busy and I'm running late. I don't have much time, but I wanted an update on the Iranian situation that we spoke about last time."

"We call it the Iranian Intervention," says Claude, swallowing. "Unfortunately, we had a minor hiccup."

President Towles looks up at him from across the coffee table, sitting exactly where he had the last time. "What do you mean a minor hiccup?"

"Well, we were unable to conclude the task with the third Iranian on our list, but I'm sending in three more teams to ensure that we get him."

President Towles winces. "Do you have any idea how fragile and precarious peace in the Middle East is, Claude? If the Iranians get any whiff of this, it'll be an international incident. It might spark war in the region and we'll have a lot of answering to do at the Security Council."

Claude nods. "Yes sir, I'm well aware of the fragility of the situation. As I said, it is a minor mistake which we're on top of. It'll be wrapped by the end of day today, our time."

Claude is lying. The three teams, Epsilon, Omicorn, and Upsilon, would only arrive in the Middle East tomorrow morning at the earliest. Latest intel had General Bukhari already in flight toward Tehran with the bodies of his assassinated colleagues, but President Towles didn't need to know that.

"You're making it very difficult for me to support your agency, Claude. If you fail, we'll have a helluva time getting any elite forces into Tehran to clean up your mess. I daresay it'll be near impossible."

Towles looks at Claude and pauses for a moment.

"If you can't complete this task by this time tomorrow, Claude, I'm pulling the plug on your agency. I don't need—and America doesn't need—a rogue agency that can't even complete simple tasks that it assigns to itself."

Claude has his hands on top of the briefcase which is on top of his lap. He bunches his right hand into a fist in frustration then quickly relaxes it. His eyes are hot coals.

"Do I make myself clear?" President Towles continues. "This country has enough spooks as it is."

"Crystal clear, Mr. President."

"Any other hiccups you'd like to get off your chest while you're at it?"

"If I might, Mr. President, NANA has an exemplary record during its seven-year history. We have accomplished close to a thousand eradications without any incident. And this Iranian Intervention was caused by circumventing the very stringent controls and rules we have in place to prevent this sort of thing. Heads will roll, Mr. President, I can promise you that."

Claude can tell that the president is not impressed. He stares blankly at Claude. "An impressive past does not ensure a potential future, Claude. If there is lack of leadership at the top, as you have just suggested, then perhaps NANA's best days are behind her. You have twenty-four hours to convince me otherwise."

Claude wasn't suggesting a lack of leadership. He just said that the rules hadn't been followed. Not that he is blameless; it is his baby after all and he should bear the brunt of the blame. Nevertheless, President Towles is being grossly unreasonable. How many incidents has the CIA botched? Claude can easily think of at least a dozen off the top of his head, and that is just in the past decade.

"I can assure you, Mr. President, by tomorrow evening, America will be a much safer place."

"I hope so, Claude, for your sake and the people whose jobs pivot upon it."

They were speaking at cross-purposes. Claude was hoping that by tomorrow morning the president would be dead. President Towles stands up, suggesting that Claude will now be leaving.

Claude stands up, holding the briefcase in his left hand. He offers out his right hand to shake the president's again. President Towles looks at it disdainfully. "This way."

The president puts his left hand behind Claude's back to usher him toward the door. Claude is starting to panic a little bit now. He has to deliver the nanos. Claude turns to look at the president as they reach the door.

Claude stops and puts his right hand on the president's shoulder and squeezes it. President Towles looks at him with a frown.

"Thank you for this second chance, Mr. President."

Claude brings his hand down along the side of the president's left upper arm, carefully, casually, just brushing his palm over the suit sleeve. He's trying to make sure thousands of nanos are littered all over the president.

"Twenty-four hours, Claude, and then NANA is no more."

Claude is shown the door.

"Twenty-four hours, Mr. President," he thinks, "and you are no more."

8:01 AM

Tehran, Iran

Armin enjoys the descent into Tehran. There is no other feeling quite like it, arriving home to the sprawling metropolis of Tehran, a city bigger than any US city, though if you asked Americans that they wouldn't know. In fact, Tehran is bigger than the biggest two cities in the US—New York and Los Angeles—combined. Armin is proud of his country and he fights for justice and truth.

And the truth is, as far as he is concerned, that Iran is not being given its due on the International stage and it is maligned—unfairly, he thought—by the Americans. How would they feel to know that Tehran's sister city is Los Angeles? There was a time when Iran was not the bogeyman it is seen as now. Armin aims to rectify that by the hand of peace, or if need be, by the sword of righteousness.

Armin hasn't slept a wink for over twenty-four hours. He is tired and he is starting to feel it. His eyelids are heavy and his mood is morose. He has been drinking espresso as if it were the fountain of youth. He is looking forward to seeing his old friend, colleague, and perhaps the only scientist in Iran who can make sense of what is happening: Dr. Usama Handal.

The president's plane slowly taxies down the runway and comes to a stop at a private hangar used for the president. This whole incident has become one of Iran's top priorities, and this is how he came to be flying home on the president's plane. His colleagues are with him, though they are in the baggage compartment in the fuselage.

Armin misses his wife and children, though he knows he will not be seeing them, not until the end of the day at least. He is scheduled for tests the whole day at Tehran University of Medical Sciences.

Armin walks off the plane and onto a mobile staircase upon which he descends. There is a government car waiting for him, and the driver is standing outside ready to open his door for him. Armin notices two police motorcycles and an ambulance to carry his deceased colleagues.

The back door opens and a short, older man with steel wool for hair empties himself out onto the tarmac. He stands up straight and walks over to Armin. He wears a thick, bushy moustache the same gray color as his hair. His eyes twinkle with warmth and kindness.

"Armin, my old friend, you look terrible," says Dr. Handal.

They embrace and kiss each other on the cheeks. Dr. Handal is thick and compact, standing below Armin's eyes. There is over ten years in age difference between the two men. They worked closely together and wore the battle scars of the Iran-Iraq war.

Even to this day, despite Tehran's modern look, you can see the decay from the war still present at the edges of the city. The whole country had been scarred as had her people. It would take a generation to fully heal. Armin and Usama would carry to the graves the horrors of the war and the ghosts of men they could not save.

"I feel like hell," says Armin.

"Come, we must get you to TUMS as soon as possible so we can determine how these Americans killed Farzan and Milad."

Usama puts his arm around Armin's shoulders and escorts him to the car. The driver opens the door for him and Armin climbs in. He feels heavy; his whole being is like a sack of half-dry cement. Every movement aches. Each breath is a heavy sigh.

Usama goes around to the driver's side and the driver opens the passenger door for him and closes it after. The driver climbs in, turns on the ignition, and soon they are on their way through the airport under police escort.

"So, you do believe it is the Americans who are trying to kill you?"

Armin nods, looking out the front through as much of the windshield as he can see. "Well, it's certainly not the Canadians, unless they've taken to killing their own." He tries a smile, but the joke seems flat and cold like stale eggs.

"You said that our Canadian business contact died the morning before you were scheduled to meet him."

"Yes, apparently it was natural causes."

"I made some inquiries with friends at the Montreal coroner's office. They told me it was sudden cardiac death. Even though this Canadian man had poor arteries, they didn't show signs of being the cause of the death. In other words, there was no atheroma or stenosis sufficient to result in cardiac arrest. More likely it seems that someone flicked the switch to his heart off."

Armin is trying to remain interested, but he is a military man, and medical matters don't make much sense to him. "If you say so Usama."

"In layman's terms, Armin, it appears that heart disease was not the cause of the Canadian's death. Now, you said you had a weird dream which awoke you. Can you explain that further?"

Armin looks over at Usama, his eyes droopy and smudged with what looks like ash.

"It's hard to explain, but I was dreaming that I was a boy of about six years old, with my father and mother and sister. We were in the desert, and toward the end of the dream we were attacked by three desert warriors. That's all background. It was the character of my father that seemed more real, more sinister than any of the others. He looked like my father, as I remember him, but I had this intense feeling that he wasn't my father, like a wolf in sheep's clothing. He seemed malevolent, like he wanted to hurt me. He seemed more real, if I can say that, than any of the other people in my dream. He toyed with his knife in a sinister way, and I felt I had no control over the outcome of this dream. I don't know if that makes sense."

Usama nods, looking forward all this time. "Dreams are strange indeed. I believe you, my friend, for I have no reason to doubt you. You said that Farzan and Milad seemed to have died at around four thirty in the morning, during sleep?"

"Yes, that's correct." Armin rubs his eyes. It feels like the backs of his eyelids are gritty sandpaper.

"Interesting. My contact in Montreal said very much the same thing. Our Canadian business contact died in his sleep."

Armin looks over at his friend. He needs to keep talking or doing something, for he fears if he doesn't, he will fall asleep, and he has never before in his life been so afraid of sleep and dreams. "How do you think this might have happened?"

Usama looks out the front window, just past the driver's right ear. He squints and purses his lips. "Well, that's an interesting question. I imagine that they've managed to do it one of two ways. The first way is to jolt the SAN, the sinoatrial node. These are a group of cells, tissue really, in the heart, or more specifically the right atrium. If you can apply a strong enough electrical charge to this tissue, you can short-circuit it. However, this approach has some drawbacks. Because the heart is so vital to an organism, there are fallback mechanisms in place. If the SAN is not functioning, then the AV node, or atrioventricular node, will provide the impulse to beat the heart. In essence, it becomes the fall pacemaker. If the AV node fails, there is a third redundancy called the Purkinje fibers which are also capable of acting as the heart's pacemaker."

Usama taps his index and middle finger of his right hand against his chin, deep in thought.

"The problem with attacking the SAN," Usama continues, "is that you really need to attack all three pacemakers at the same time. You need to short-circuit them simultaneously, otherwise there is a great chance one of the three will survive to maintain the heart's rhythm."

Armin is looking at Usama. In his ears and in his heart he can hear his own heart beating like a drum. But it sounds like someone is banging too forcefully on that drum of his heart. His beat is heavy. His heart feels like a frightened bird flapping about in a cage too small.

"What's the other method?" Armin asks.

Usama looks at him and puts his hands in his lap. He looks down at them. "The second way is through the medulla. This is the part of the brainstem that is tasked with the autonomic or involuntary nerve functions of the body. Things like heart rhythm, breathing, and things like that. Most folks realize that the heart is capable of beating without nerve impulse or signals from the brain. However, if you wanted to be sure of short-circuiting the whole heart at once, you could send such an impulse from the medulla—if you knew what you were doing."

"What is your best guest if you had to make a guess right now?"

Usama looks at his friend. His eyes are wet but still bright with kindness.

"If it were me. If I were trying to kill people in their sleep, I would do it through the medulla. Autopsying the brain is difficult, more difficult than the heart, and using the medulla would offer greater control over shorting out the heart if that was what you wanted to do, and it would make it look natural. There would be no signs to suggest that the heart was stopped unnaturally. And knowing that everyone who has ended up dead in so far died in their sleep makes me think that everything is being controlled through the brain."

"But how? How could they control our brains without us knowing?"

"That is the question we need to find the answer to. Do you remember anything unusual the day before Farzan and Milad died? Anything at all? Were you attacked? Did someone brush into you more harshly than seemed reasonable? Did you cut yourself on anything?"

Armin thinks for a moment. That day before they died, nothing really happened. It was a pleasant day. Then he remembers.

"Well, I don't know, this hardly seems worth mentioning."

"Anything at this stage, Armin, is worth mentioning."

"Well, there was a cloud of mosquitoes that descended upon us as we sat down to eat at an outside restaurant in Lisbon. They seemed unusual, but I just figured that's because they were Portuguese mosquitoes."

"What do you mean they seemed unusual?"

"I don't know really. I didn't pay them much attention, but they sounded—they sounded more like machines, like sewing machines rather than mosquitoes. Just seemed strange."

"Did all of you get bitten?"

"Yes, we did, but that doesn't seem unusual does it?"

"Well, think. What else happened during that time?"

Armin's brain is foggy. He is finding it hard to concentrate. It was only a couple of days ago yet it seems like Lisbon was years away.

"Um, Milad got up to talk to this woman who came in and sat at the table next to us. She sounded American, wore dark glasses, and she was quite attractive if I recall. She rebuffed him and then she left."

"Did she eat anything? Did she leave before or after you got bitten?"

"Uh, it was after we got bitten, and no, she didn't eat anything or order anything for that matter. I just figured Milad had upset her."

"That's interesting. Anything else that seems unusual?"

"Well, now that you mention it. Just a small thing, but it seemed like the mosquitoes just vanished moments after we got bitten."

"And you never noticed any other mosquitoes or bugs the rest of the day?"

"No, I didn't."

"Hmm," says Usama, grimacing.

"I don't like that look," says Armin.

"You know, my friend, the Chinese have for the past decade or more been trying to work on nanotechnology. So have the Americans. The idea is that you can create little robots, about the size of a cell—at least that is the dream—that can be injected into a person and they can do such things as clean out arteries, monitor vitals, and things like that. But the Chinese, and I imagine the Americans, have been trying to develop nano soldiers. Little robots that can be injected into a person and incapacitate them. But this has all been theory and science fiction. Maybe it is no longer so."

"You mean there might be American robot soldiers inside me, trying to kill me as we speak?"

Armin swallows and it feels like a stone that got stuck in his throat. He is no longer scared. He is horrified and he wants to crawl out of his skin.

"Perhaps."

1:01 AM

Run-Down Industrial Plant, Outside Washington, D.C.

Claude sits in the control room, tapping his fingers nervously along the desk. Everything has been set up just as it should have. He has verified that the nanos have attached themselves to President Towles.

As soon as he got back to his office, he fired up his laptop, which he seldom uses, and awakened his sleeping nanos. He stayed mesmerized at his computer, watching them work their way into the president's system.

He didn't actually watch them. They didn't have cameras attached. Rather he watched the computer feedback as the nanos made their way through his jacket and shirt and into his skin. It only took them thirty-seven minutes to get through his clothing and onto his skin.

Another thirteen minutes and they were placed all over his brain and nervous system like good little stealth soldiers awaiting orders from command.

In front of Claude is a holographic screen with read-outs from several of the nanobots. He knows the president is sleeping because he tried to see what the president could see and was met with an error message. Kathleen was with him and told him the message meant that the target was asleep.

Yolanda is here too. She is fidgeting and chewing on her lip absentmindedly. What they are about to attempt is high-stakes. If it doesn't work, they'll all be screwed and thrown in jail forever. That scares her. She also has misgivings about killing the president of the United States.

But she was with Claude during that first meeting. She knows her job depends on a more sympathetic president. But more than that, she trusts Claude. He is the most patriotic American she has ever met. His patriotism is a fervor, a burning fire in his soul, a conviction so certain it is only shared with the religious and insane.

But she knows he isn't insane. She has never met a man more intelligent, more confident in his outlook and concern with bringing America back to its glory days. She would follow him to the ends of the earth. She knows that he knows that what he is doing is for the good of the many, and sometimes the few are sacrificed, even if they're the top of the heap.

Still, they need to pull it off or nobody in America will ever be safe again from tyranny, terrorism, and poverty. She doesn't want to imagine an America without NANA succeeding.

Only Claude and Yolanda know who today's target is. Kathleen doesn't, and she doesn't want to know. She is smart enough to realize that she might have qualms with some of the targets that NANA goes after, so she'd just as soon not know. But she comforts herself with the fact that, unlike many of the other government agencies, NANA never tortures anyone.

They assassinate quickly, swiftly, and arguably painlessly, and with those thoughts she sleeps very well at night. The paycheck doesn't hurt either.

The control room is at the opposite end of the R&D section, separated by a hall and offices. Beyond the control room are seven adjoining rooms. Small. This is where the agents can carry out their tasks. This is where Tomo Daisen will assassinate the president from.

The Industrial Plant, as it is colloquially known amongst those that work here, is empty. The scientists work regular hours. Kathleen is here because Claude requested her and because she's getting paid ten thousand dollars for tonight's event. Snipers are here 24/7. Tyrell has gone home, but in his place is another security officer named John "JT" Johnson.

Additionally, Claude has brought in another three armed agents to offer security in the bowels just in case anything goes wrong. This assassination is going to happen or nobody is getting out of here alive. These are the kinds of sacrifices that Claude is willing to make to ensure a brighter future for America and, extending from that, the world.

Kathleen looks over at Claude, who still drums his fingers upon the tabletop.

"These are good numbers," she says, pointing at the holographic screen in front of them. "Should be easy to get in and out when he enters REM."

"How do you know the target is a he?"

"Or she. I was just assuming."

Claude offers a wince as a smile.

Kathleen says, "Tonight's target is a big fish, I guess?"

It was a question. Claude looks at her for a moment, searching her face. Her face is calm and kind. She's trying to break the ice; she can feel the tension. She doesn't want to know the details.

"Well, I'll put it this way, Kathleen. World peace, America's dominance, and the continuation of NANA all rely on this eradication going as smoothly as possible." Claude pauses for emphasis. "And I don't exaggerate when I say that."

Out in the hallway, Claude hears commotion. There is a knock at the door. JT opens it and pops his head in.

"Sir, Alpha Team is here."

"Let them in," says Claude.

Anthony Buckles, James Seaton, Margaret Rakes, and finally Tomo Daisen walk into the room. They all feel sheepish, like they've been sent to the principal's office.

"Take a seat around the table for a moment," says Claude.

Claude taps at the table in front of him and the holographic screen shows a different image of vitals and other text, projected this time on the one-way mirror that looks into the Theta rooms. Off to one corner is a small table where the four of them sit down. Tom is watching Claude carefully. He has great admiration for this man who founded NANA, but lately his zeal has seemed irrational.

"Lady and gentlemen," says Claude. "Tonight is an opportunity for you to redeem Alpha Team if you wish for Alpha Team to remain a viable team here at NANA."

Claude stands up and walks over toward them. He pauses and looks over each of them one at a time.

"Yes, we do," says Anthony. "On behalf of all of us, I'm terribly sorry for the mishap. Please be assured it won't happen again."

Claude grins. "You're right. It won't happen again because you have only tonight to prove yourselves. There was a gross negligence of protocol, and all of you are aware of the rules, so you all bear responsibility. You, Tom, perhaps most of all."

Tom looks up at him. Tom's hands are clasped in front of him on the desk. On his red t-shirt is a sketch of the smiling Buddha. Tom's not smiling, though. He loves his job, he loves keeping America safe, and, although he thinks Claude's being a little unkind, he realizes he needs to make this right.

"It won't happen again," says Tom sincerely, looking at Claude.

"Good, because although I'm impressed you managed two hits in one night, that's not how we do things. And we do things the way we do so that there are no mistakes. As it stands, NANA is in a precarious position because of this."

Claude turns and looks at the projected screen on the window. He points at it.

"This here," he says, "is General Armin Bukhari, and he is undergoing tests. They're keeping him from REM sleep so that we can't get to him. Do you see the problem here? If they find these nanos, if they find just a trace of them, or in the other two, it will be an international catastrophe."

Everyone is staring at the screen. Armin is asleep, but far from REM. His vitals look excited, but that's to be expected from lack of deep sleep.

"But what's done is done. They won't be able to pin anything on us or America. The blame can be put on the Portuguese or the Canadians because they were never even in our country. Nevertheless, this is not a mistake I will tolerate again."

Claude turns back to them. "Tom, you will erase tonight's target. This cannot fail. I don't care who you think it is once you get there, you will complete your mission. Is that understood?"

Tom nods.

"Let me be clear. No one leaves here until this mission is accomplished."

Tom looks at Claude and thinks the man has gone a little off. Of course he'll complete the mission; that's what he's trained to do. Making threats like Claude has is not necessary. Tom is not one to usually question his orders. He's a career military man; his oath is to his country.

"Is that really necessary?" asks Anthony. "I mean, this is Alpha Team and we're highly trained and capable."

Claude shoots him a stern look. "That's what I thought until the last debacle. Now I need assurances, and those three men out there are my assurances."

That shuts Anthony up.

"We'll complete this mission, sir," says James, "if I have to do it myself."

"That's the spirit. Speaking of you, James. Once Tom has finished with the main target, you'll finish up with Armin if he enters REM, which he is bound to do within the next few hours, if the Iranians will allow him to live."

Claude looks over at the four of them. "Any questions?" he asks.

Anthony puts ups his hand.

"Yes, Anthony?"

"Do you mind telling us who the main target is?"

"Yes I do. This one is top-secret, and to ensure it stays that way, we've encoded additional algorithms to ensure that the target is not identified inside dreamscape with their actual image."

Kathleen looks up at Claude with a quizzical look. He shoots her a glare and she looks away. What he's just said is a lie. They can not manipulate the dreamscape and the target's dreamscape avatar that way.

"Fair enough," says Anthony.

"Anything else?"

James shakes his head, Margaret looks down.

"Let's get it done then," says Tom.

Claude smiles. "Go and get ready."

1:43 AM

Run-Down Industrial Plant, Outside Washington, D.C.

Tom is ready in the Theta room. It is small and seems a little cramped. Not much bigger than a hospital room. Inside there is the bed upon which he now sits with a blanket and pillow, though the room is warm and he'll unlikely need the blanket. Next to the bed is a bank of electronic equipment and computers which will be attached to him as soon as he's ready.

Tom is only in blue boxer briefs. His socks, red sneakers, red t-shirt, and blue jeans are folded up on a chair across from the computer equipment. Margaret walks in to check in on him.

"How are you doing?" she asks.

He smiles at her and nods. His hands are holding the edges of the bed on either side of his legs. "Good. I'd like to get this whole thing behind us and move on from the hiccup."

"Sounds like they don't consider it a minor hiccup."

"You're right, but these things happen in love and war—more the war part."

He looks at her and grins. She smiles back at him. She loves his laid-back way, the twinkle in his dark brown eyes, and his unkempt but rakish black hair glinting in the light with silver flashes. Margaret looks down and the smile drops off her face.

"Are you feeling confident about tonight?"

"With you as my controller, I'm always confident."

She smiles again. "We really need this to go smoothly, or we'll all likely be out of work by the morning."

"By morning, we'll be all fast asleep dreaming of a job well done."

There's a rap on the one-way-mirrored window. Margaret looks over at it out of habit even though she can't see anything behind it.

"I think the target has entered REM. Who do you think it is?" she asks.

"I don't know and I don't care. I just want to wrap this up and put Alpha Team back in its right place as the best."

Tom lies down and Margaret busies herself with attaching the electrodes to him.

"Do you need any help with this one?" she asks.

He looks at her. A frown has worried her face like thin worms on her forehead.

"No, thanks. I've got this."

"Okay."

She finishes up and checks that the computers are all running and reading his signals correctly. She's satisfied and turns to leave, but hesitates. She comes back to him. He is lying on his back staring at the ceiling. Already she can tell his heart rate is slowing and he's beginning his meditative process. She leans in close to his face and whispers in his ear.

"I think Mr. Martin is lying. I don't think they can reimage anybody in the dreams, so who you see as your target is your target. Let me know who it is? I'm curious."

"Okay," he whispers back.

"Good luck," she says. And she hesitates again. She wants to kiss him on the cheek. She wants to lie down next to him and curl up against him. She can feel the heat coming off from his body. She can smell his scent. It's hard to describe, it's clean and fresh, with woody, musky and citrus notes from his cologne. She inhales deeply and then pulls away. She pats his hand.

She walks out and into the control room. Claude, Anthony, James, and Yolanda are standing against the window like gargoyles.

"What did you say to him?" asks Claude. He's annoyed because he couldn't hear it from the microphones in the Theta room.

"Oh, that. I just wished him good luck and reminded him how important it is that we succeed."

Claude nods. He hopes she's telling the truth. Though what else she might have said eludes him.

"Target has entered REM," says Anthony. His voice is firm and brittle, barely coming out of his mouth without breaking. She knows he needs a win on this one or heads will roll. Problem is, his head will be amongst them.

Margaret takes a seat by her station and taps at the desk. A keyboard comes to life under her fingers and she starts tapping away at it, bringing to life all the vitals of Tom as well as information from both his and the target's nanos.

"I'm ready," she says.

"Good," says Claude.

He looks at Kathleen and nods at her. Kathleen heads over to where Margaret is and stands behind her, watching her closely and supervising the process and algorithms on the holographic screen in front of them.

Margaret feels like a schoolgirl who's being held in detention.

"Tom is entering Theta," she says. "He should be inside dreamscape any moment."

"Prime Minister Hoshi, please come this way."

Tom is looking at a secret service man who is leading him down a hallway. He thinks he's in the White House—at least, that's how it looks like to him from all the movies he's seen.

He's following two secret service men and just behind Tom are two other security officers. Tom has a feeling these two are here to protect him—or her, as is the case now. Tom passes a mirror along the hallway and looks into it. He sees an older woman in her mid to late fifties, slim, attractive for her age, and about five feet two inches tall. Her hair is straight and short. He realizes he's the first female prime minister of Japan, Kaho Hoshi.

Tom looks around but he can't seem to identify his target. This is unusual; usually the target is already present when he enters the dream. Seldom does he enter a dreamscape where the target is not there.

They turn right and enter into an office and walk through that into another office.

"Prime Minister, the President of the United States of America," says the one security officer.

"Prime Minister, so good of you to come. We have lots to talk about," says the president, offering his hand. Tom shakes it. He notices that he is dressed in a navy skirt suit. His hands—the woman's hands—are immaculate, soft and well manicured.

"It is my pleasure, President Towles. I am looking forward to continuing our good relations between our two countries."

Tom waves off the two security officers and the POTUS waves off the two secret service agents. The door closes behind them and it is just the two of them in the room. Then Tom notices it for the first time, the blinking blue beacon growing from the inside of President Towles head.

At first he ignores it. It must be wrong, but then it grows larger and it is definitely coming from the President.

"Please sit down," says the president.

Toms sits down across from the president and leans over to one side to be certain that there isn't someone else intertwined with the president's avatar. There is no one else there. They are the only two in this room. Alone.

"Surely, they are mad to be trying to assassinate the president," thinks Tom. "This must be a mistake."

The president is talking to him, but Tom has tuned him out. Tom stands up and walks around behind the president. He's surveying the room. This is a very mundane, realistic dreamscape. Nobody is in here but the two of them. Tom walks around to the front of the president again. The blue beacon keeps blinking, growing bigger and then smaller from inside the president's head. There is no doubt. This is his target.

"Prime Minister, are you okay?"

"Oh, sorry. I'm not feeling very well."

"Can I have anything brought in for you?"

Tom waves off the gesture. "Can I really assassinate the president," he thinks. "It's preposterous. I can't do it. Claude must think I'm mad if he thinks I'll do it."

But what can he do? Tom realizes that if he doesn't kill the president, he himself is as good as dead. Claude told him nobody's getting out until this job has been done. But he knows he can't do it. He swore an oath of enlistment, which in part has him obey the orders of the president, and surely the president would not require his own assassination. He also has to protect the Constitution from enemies both foreign and domestic.

"Prime Minister, please sit down."

Tom sits down and smiles at the president. "What I'm about to tell you, you must listen to very carefully," he says.

The president frowns.

"You are in grave danger. There are domestic enemies who are trying to kill you."

The president stands up. "Prime Minister, clearly you are not well."

Tom stands up and grabs the president's lapels. He shakes him.

"I am serious, Mr. President. There are those who are trying to kill you." Tom slaps him across the face. "This is a dream, you need to wake up and stay awake. Wake up."

Tom slaps him again. The president is horrified he is backing away with Tom still holding onto him, slapping him every so often.

"Help!" the president yells. "Help!"

The two secret service agents enter through the door with their handguns drawn. Tom extracts himself from the dreamscape.

"What am I going to do?" he thinks, listening to the low hum coming from the computers in the room with him.

2:01 AM

Run-Down Industrial Plant, Outside Washington, D.C.

Tom lies still for a moment. He's no longer in the dreamscape, and he wonders why they want the president killed. But that's a question he'll get the answer to much later. He's out of dreamscape which means he's no longer in Theta and they'll know it any moment, if they haven't already figured it out.

"I'll pretend everything happened according to plan," he thinks. Tom gets up and yanks the electrodes off himself. He looks up at the one-way mirror.

"EOL confirmed?" he asks.

He reaches over for his clothes and starts getting dressed. Inside the control room, Maggie looks at the computer read-out. Nothing's happened, and Tom came out of Theta too early. She doesn't know what's going on, but the way Tom is behaving, something doesn't seem right.

"Well, do we have EOL confirmation or not?" asks Claude looking back at her.

Maggie taps away at the keyboard below her and the screen goes black. She's created a mini diversion, put a wrench in the machine. Kathleen still looks over her shoulder.

"Woops, I accidentally closed the program. It'll just be a moment. Sorry, about that," Maggie says.

Claude turns away from the one-way mirror and comes around to stand behind Maggie to see for himself. Maggie starts up the computer software again, trying to take her time without showing them she's taking her time.

"Did you see anything?" Claude asks Kathleen.

"No, sorry. I couldn't tell one way or the other."

Tom enters the control room from the Theta room. "Well?" he asks, pretending to be frustrated. "Can I get EOL confirmation so James can get ready for his bit?"

Tom comes around to where Claude and Kathleen are standing behind Maggie.

"I know I erased the president," says Tom, loud enough so that Maggie can hear.

Claude shoots him a look. "I told you, we can reimage the avatars on the dreamscape," he says, seething under his breath.

But there's something about the tone in his voice that Maggie doesn't believe. She's never seen any memo or research to suggest it's possible, and the way he denies it just confirms it for her. Inside she's horrified they tried to get Tom to murder the president. She can't imagine any reason under heaven for that kind of a task. She looks at the holographic image. The algorithm is coming back online. Tom's nano is feeding information first.

"I just want confirmation of EOL," says Tom, backing away just slightly behind Claude.

James and Anthony and Yolanda are now crowding around looking at the holographic screen too. Tom backs away farther until he can feel the door behind him with his hands. He starts to open it slowly, and just as he steps out into the hallway without anyone noticing, he hears Kathleen.

"This doesn't look like EOL to me."

"I'm sorry, sir. Nobody's allowed out here without Mr. Martin," says the soldier.

Tom sizes him up. He's about 6 feet and 180 pounds. His two colleagues are practically the same size. He can tell they're well-trained soldiers, perhaps marines. He'd like to make this less awkward for all of them.

"I know, but I got permission from the teacher for a washroom break. You know how many cups of coffee a guy's gotta drink to stay alert on this kind of shift?"

Tom offers a big grin. The soldier starts to smile, which means he's lost concentration on the task at hand. Tom takes this as his opportunity. He palms him in the nose. This is unexpected and the soldier grunts while loosening the grip on his M4. Tom snatches it from his hand. While the first soldier is stumbling back, there's a split second where Tom has the upper hand. He uses this fraction of time to ram the stock of the M4 into the second soldier's throat. This man buckles, gasping for breath and clutching at his throat.

By now Tom has lost the element of surprise. The third soldier is bringing his M4 up as he steps back to gain space and distance. Tom sweeps the soldier's front foot out from under him and this unbalances the man. Tom steps in as the soldier is wobbling and slams the butt against his temple. The soldier is out before he hits the floor. Tom quickly drags him against the door just as James tries to open it.

"You better get in here, Tom!" he hears James yelling.

Tom runs off still holding the M4. He might need its help on the way out. He jumps into one of the lifts that is still open. Thank God it doesn't require the same security redundancies as required to get down here. He pushes the button. It's the only button in here, and it takes him to the main floor.

"Goddamn!" yells Claude. "James, get in here and get ready to finish what Tom started."

"Yes sir."

The first soldier with the bloody nose drags his semi-conscious colleague out of the way and opens the door.

"Sir, do you want me to go after him?"

Claude turns back, a sneer on his face. "No, but you better damn well make sure no one else gets out of here alive unless I say so. Do you understand, soldier?"

"Yes sir. Sorry, sir."

Claude strides over to a telephone attached to the far end of the wall along with a panel of screens that show the CCTVs situated all over this building. He wishes he had control over the elevators from here, but he doesn't. Fire code and all that bullshit. He picks up the phone. A man on the other end answers.

"Yes sir?"

"JT, listen carefully. Tomo Daisen is coming up unauthorized. Do you understand? You will stop him from leaving us by any means necessary. Use deadly force if you have to. Do you understand?"

"Uh, yes sir, any means necessary."

"Good, your job depends on it."

Claude hangs up, more forcefully than he needs to. He turns around and looks at everyone in the control room.

"Nobody else is leaving until we've finished what we've started. Am I clear?"

Mumbles and nods all around. Maggie can't believe what she's gotten herself into. She can't be party to a presidential assassination. Not just because of the consequences, but because it isn't right. But if she tries to leave, she'll be shot. She's as good as dead if she leaves, but if she stays she'll have to live with her conscience for the rest of her life. But she might be able to live to help Tom another day. "Who am I kidding?" she thinks to herself. "Tom's not going to make it out of here alive, not with all those snipers up top." She feels like crying, but that's not going to help anyone.

"Get to work!" demands Claude.

James heads into a different Theta room from the one Tom used. He doesn't want to use the same room as that bastard coward.

The elevator starts to slow. Tom's trying to remember how many snipers he saw on the way here. He should have been more observant. He knows there are at least six of them, but he only remembers seeing three. One in each corner up by the ceiling.

The elevator stops and opens up. He's inside an old grain silo. It's a small one, made of metal and about ten feet high. He's got to move quickly. The sniper's bullets are probably armor-piercing and will cut through both him and the silo as if they were made of paper. Tom opens the door and runs for the nearest farm equipment, which he remembers was an old tractor.

He takes cover behind the engine block. He sees the sweep of red laser sights and the pinging of bullets against the tractor. The whole building comes to life with the cacophony of machine gunfire. Tom can tell they've selected three-round bursts. A bullet skips across the concrete floor just to his right.

Tom slips out to the right of the engine block and sends a three-round burst up toward the ceiling. He marked well, and a sniper falls from the catwalk and camouflage up there. The others open fire again and Tom crouches around behind. None of the bullets are tearing through metal that is thicker than an eighth of an inch. They aren't armor-piercing, which he's grateful for.

Tom has to make it out. He mentally takes note of where a second sniper is. It's dark in here, not pitch black; the lights are on but they're very dim. He marks in his mind where the muzzle flashes are coming from. Tom peeks around the other side of the engine block, quickly sights, and pulls the trigger. He hits his mark. Another sniper falls down.

The front entrance is practically the furthest point from him in this building. And they'll be expecting him to try for it. But the rear entrance, which is locked—he knows because he tried it when he arrived—is only about fifteen feet away from him. And the two snipers that would have the best shot at it are now dead.

Tom looks back toward the rear entrance. It has some cover. There are some chunks of farm equipment surrounding it. It isn't a door that is used often. He turns back to take in the rest of the building. He fires a few rounds up toward the ceiling. He's trying to draw fire to figure out where the others are.

Fire is returned. There is one more sniper that has a good angle on the rear door. But Tom doesn't have a good shot of him from where he is. Tom makes a sprint off to his right diagonally, diving and rolling behind a bulldozer's blade, unattached to the bulldozer, as bullets bite and spit behind him.

Tom steadies himself, spins up, and fires up toward the sniper who will have the best shot at him when he gets to the rear entrance. He pulls the trigger twice, but he's high and then too low. He doesn't hit him. Tom's wasting time. He knows he is. The longer you're in a firefight, the greater your chances of getting hit. The increasing likelihood of loss.

Tom looks around to his left. He's got a clean line of fire at the rear door. He aims carefully and fires three rounds. They hit the latch. It looks like he's broken the lock, but he's not certain. More sniper fire chews up around him and pings off the metal blade he lies behind. Tom aims again and fires three more bullets at the door latch, just for good measure.

The problem is that he's now given up his avenue of escape. Still, he has no other choice. He can't see himself getting to the front door; that's suicide. The back door is at least possible if he's quick about it.

Tom get's ready, crouching. He pulls his M4 up and sprays bullets toward the ceiling carelessly. He squeezes three sets of three out and then launches himself toward the door. His mag is now empty. He doesn't have to wait long for the line of fire to follow him, like burning fire ants; they chew away at his heels.

Tom slams himself into the door. It gives but it doesn't open. He leans back and slams at it again. It gives way. As he stumbles outside, he feels a hot poker thrust through his side. He winces. He knows he's been hit, but he keeps running. At least he can run. That means it hasn't hit nerves or spine.

He gets to his car and throws the M4 in the passenger seat. He fumbles for his keys from his pocket and starts up his blue '67 Camaro. He knows they don't have line of fire because he's too close to the building, but once he gets out they might. But he's more worried about some of the snipers rappelling down and coming out after him. That won't take them long.

Tom sucks his breath through a thin wire. He winces. The pain is biting and hot along his left side. The Camaro roars to life.

"Sorry, baby," he says. "She's about to get chewed up too," he thinks.

The rear wheels spin for a moment, creating loud plumes of dirt clouds before she bites into the dusty road and he guns her out of there. As he comes around the front of the building, JT is waiting and opens fire. The side of his Camaro gets pockmarked by .223s. Tom is scrunching down as best he can, and the last thing he sees out the rearview is muzzle flashes from the windows at the top of the building, muzzle flashes from JT, and two more snipers running out the front door.

Tom's on the main road driving like a madman. He winces. He puts his hand down to touch his side. It's a through and through—that's good. There's blood, but not a ton, which means they probably didn't get the kidney. He's trying to decide if he should head to the hospital, but they'll be waiting for him, he's sure. Besides, there's someplace first he's gotta go.

6:47 PM

Tehran University of Medical Sciences, Tehran, Iran

Armin's world is a thick fog of confusion. He's been through test after test here at TUMS and it all seems like a blur. He's lost consciousness for periods of time but he doesn't think he was sleeping. It didn't feel like sleep. This unconsciousness is more like being drugged and dragged down cold sewers where Zahhak and his minions poke and prod.

Armin's eyes feel heavy and sticky, like two iron balls coated in honey and dipped in sand. He looks around and sees he's in a private hospital room. He can't remember how he got here, but he thinks he remembers a pretty nurse leaning over him as they rolled him in. He wants to speak with Usama and hear some good news. Armin thinks he remembers Usama mentioning he'll be in shortly to see him.

But was that a dream, and if not, how long ago was it? Armin has lost all track of time. Across from his bed is an analog clock and it looks like it's reading ten to seven, but his eyes are blurry and he's looking through Vaseline.

Armin closes his eyes. He's given up trying not to fall asleep. He doesn't care anymore, if sleep drowns him in the river of death, so be it. Anything for a moment's peaceful respite. And he closes his eyes, and it soothes the grittiness and cools his hot orbs. But as hard as he tries, he just cannot fall asleep.

Outside, Armin thinks he hears voices. He is not mistaken. His wife, Soraya, enters with his oldest daughter, Jaleh. Armin wiggles his way farther up the bed. His eyelids are heavy and they close over his eyes like slipping coins. He is doing his best to keep them open.

"Daddy," says Jaleh, coming over to the side of the bed where she hugs her father and kisses him on the cheek.

"My beautiful daughter," says Armin, "and my lovely wife. I didn't think I'd be seeing you so soon."

Soraya comes to sit on the side of the bed and kisses her husband on the lips. "Usama called and said we could come and see you. And we wanted to. I wanted to hear all about your trip to Canada, but apparently it didn't go very well."

Armin shakes his head. It seems so far away, but it was only a few days ago. "I think the Americans are trying to kill us."

Soraya looks worried. She looks down and fidgets with her hands. Armin reaches over with his left hand and places it on top of hers. He notices an IV tube coming out of his wrist entering a bag somewhere up by his head.

"What about Baraz?" Armin asks. "Is he coming?"

Soraya nods her head. "He is just finishing up an important meeting with the Chinese. He's doing very well in the government, as you know. He says he'll be right over when he's finished with them."

Armin nods. He is proud of all his children. His firstborn, Baraz; his oldest daughter, who sits on his bed opposite from his wife, who is studying medicine at this very university. And then there is Javed, his youngest son, studying engineering at Cambridge, and Mahine, the artist in the family; she is studying music at Oxford. He is proud of them all.

"Do not worry Mahine and Javed," he says.

"Too late," says Soraya, smiling at her husband. "They're both coming on the earliest flight this weekend."

Armin smiles at her. This is why he loves her. She has always put her family first and loves him with all of her heart. The children too. As he looks at his oldest daughter and his wife who he's loved for almost thirty years, he feels his heart warm and his mind at peace.

"Usama said we shouldn't stay too long. He'll be along soon. He says you need to get some proper rest." Soraya looks at Armin nervously. "What have they done to you?" She looks back down at her hands. She is nervous and scared for her husband, for herself.

Armin takes her hands in both of his and squeezes them gently. "Do not be scared, my love. Allah is great. Allah is merciful. It is in Allah's hand now, and Usama is the best doctor we have in Iran. He will take care of us."

Soraya looks up at her husband and smiles. But she smiles through a veil of tears. Her eyes are wet and damp. She has never questioned her husband and his loyalty to Iran, but her worst fears now seem to be coming true. That his work as a military man will be the cause of his death.

"But to answer your question," Armin continues, "it appears that the Americans have been working on nanotechnology. Little robots"—he brings his index finger and thumb together, almost touching—"that are the size of a cell. Farzan, Milad, and I seem to have been bitten by what appeared to be mosquitoes, and maybe they were, but we think that's how they got these little robots into us."

"Can they not get them out?"

"Usama thinks that is possible, or if not to actually get them out, to disable them somehow, but he needs to find them first, and you can imagine how difficult this is with something so small. But have faith, my love. I am certain Usama will find them and disable them."

She has known Armin for almost thirty years, since they were young and the world seemed full of potential. They met here in Tehran at the University. He was studying politics and she science. And in all these years, she has come to know him as if he were part of her. And she can tell now that he means what he says, but his belief in it is not certain. This worries her more. But she will not tell him.

"He is the best doctor, my husband. He will find out how to fix you."

Armin smiles and looks over at Jaleh. "You are not worried. My oldest daughter who studies medicine, you know how good Doctor Handal is, don't you?"

"I am a little worried, Daddy," she says. "Even though Doctor Handal's reputation is unsurpassed, the Americans worry me with their technology and military budget."

"But these are such small things, Jaleh; they are almost harmless."

"Don't belittle the danger, Daddy, please. They killed General Najafi and Doctor Saatchi, and I don't want them to kill you."

There is a knock on the partially open door and Doctor Handal pokes his head around before walking in.

"I am glad to see your family here with you, Armin." He walks up to Soraya and they hug and kiss on the cheeks. He does the same with Jaleh.

"You know," Usama says, "Jaleh's professors tell me she is going to make a very fine physician. Perhaps I will hire you when you are finished."

Usama smiles broadly at Jaleh as her eyes light up.

"That would be a great honor, Doctor Handal," she says.

Usama is standing just off the side of the bed on Armin's right. A stethoscope hangs around his neck like a frayed scarf.

"Have you found these little robots in my husband?" Soraya asks.

Usama looks at her in the eyes and slowly shakes his head. "I have not. At least, not yet. But I am very hopeful. I have arranged the MRI for later this evening, which I think will help us. In the meantime, I am going to help the pathologist as we work on General Najafi and Doctor Saatchi. It should be much easier to uncover these little devils through dissection than on a live person, though it might still take time."

"How much time, Doctor?"

"Hours at least."

"And when you find them?" asks Soraya, trying to remain hopeful.

"Then I think the best approach is to try and figure out the frequency they are on, and through that frequency we should be able to shut them down, and with a bit of luck, once we have shut them down, the body should be able to identify them as a pathogen and, within a day or so, eliminate them from Armin's body."

"Thank you, Doctor," says Jaleh. "I know you are doing everything for my father."

Usama smiles at Jaleh and then at Soraya. "I will take the best care of Armin that I can. I have known him since we were young. He is like a younger brother to me. But for now we must let him get proper rest."

"Is that not dangerous?" asks Soraya.

"Yes, Soraya, it is a little dangerous because that is how we think the robots attack, but he needs proper sleep or he could become mentally impaired, and that would be worse. We will be watching his vitals very closely, and if anything seems out of the ordinary we will bring him out. But he needs at least a few hours before irreparable damage is caused."

Soraya nods.

Usama continues, "The nurses will be here shortly to detach the IV, which is keeping him from deep sleep, and they will attach electrodes to monitor all his vitals. Nurses will be watching from their station every second. I have told them the severity of this. We will do everything we can to keep him alive. You of course can stay with him and watch over him too."

"I would like that, Doctor," says Soraya.

"I will stay too," says Jaleh.

"Then I have nothing to be concerned about," says Usama. "How do you feel Armin?"

"I will be glad to get some sleep. As I told Soraya, it is in Allah's hands now."

"With my help," says Usama, smiling.

2:30 AM

Washington, D.C.

Tom realizes he is no longer being followed, so he slows down to the speed limit. He doesn't need to deal with cops on top of everything else that's happened tonight. Along a dark, dimly lit street he edges onto the side of the road away from a light pole. The darkest part of the street. Tom can't see any traffic in either direction. He pops the trunk.

He climbs out of the car. The effort makes him wince. He needs to have his bullet wound looked at. He knows it's not fatal, but it could end up that way if it doesn't get seen too. He's seen gangrene in the desert and it isn't pretty.

Tom walks around to the other side of the car and opens up the passenger door. He braces himself with his hand against the roof. Bending shoots pain up and down his torso from the wound, a radiation of pain that grips him like a vice. Tom takes a last look up and down the highway. There is still no traffic. He grabs the M4 and carries it carelessly to the back of the car.

He tosses the M4 into the car. It's not good to him now. He can't use it except as a bat, and if it gets seen on his passenger seat, he'll be in worse trouble than it's worth. He curses under his breath. He should have counted and been more frugal with the rounds in his M4. If he had some rounds left, the carbine could be more valuable.

Tom slams the trunk down, just as a semi comes around a corner and into view about a half mile away. He's thankful he's wearing a red t-shirt; it's harder to see that he's bleeding through it. Might look like he just spilled something on it. Tom gingerly lowers himself back into the driver's seat as the truck races by.

He leans across the gearshift over to the passenger side, bracing himself on his right elbow to ease the pain. He opens the glove box and pulls out his 1911. It's fully loaded, and there are two more mags he leaves in the glove box. He tucks it with difficulty and shooting pain in the back of his waistband.

Tom looks at the clock on the dash. It's 2:35. He doesn't know how things are going back in NANA's bowels, but one thing Tom does know is that James probably doesn't have any qualms about killing the president. He's an old-school soldier that way, always following orders without critical thought.

"I've gotta get going," he says to himself, and he guns it, spitting up gravel and plums of dust on this dark, practically deserted stretch of highway with the lights of Washington bright before him.

"Is he in Theta yet?" growls Claude.

He's pissed off. He's trying to remain calm, but the last few days have pushed his buttons like they've never been pushed before. First, it was the president. He could live with that; the man was unpatriotic and an asshole. That happens. But now, what should have been a brilliant plan to set up Alpha Team, and especially Tom, has gone to shit. He is fighting against time. Still, Claude doesn't think it is a fair fight; he figures time is on his side. And he is probably right.

Claude thinks that Tom is heading to the White House. He's right, and he tries to imagine what that will look like. His security team informed him they had hit Tom. They didn't know how badly, but it was a body shot. If they were lucky, Tom will bleed out before he gets anywhere near the White House.

But let's imagine he does get there, thinks Claude. He's going to look like a raving lunatic at 3 AM or so trying to convince security guards that the president is about to be assassinated. No, Claude likes his chances. But he's still pissed off. All of this should have been smoother than it's ended up.

Margaret is looking over Kathleen's shoulder. Kathleen has taken over as controller on this mission. Margaret is watching. She's glad she's been recused. At least her hands won't be as sullied as if she were actually at the controls. It's a small mercy.

"James has entered Theta," says Kathleen, her eyes glued to the screen in front of her.

Margaret looks through the one-way mirror and sees James lying down in the corpse pose, as they call it in yoga. He's a decade or more older than Tom and it shows. His brush-cut military hairstyle is mostly gray. What was brown hair has now tarnished a steely gray. His face is lined and his body is sinewy, not the smooth ripples of taut muscle that she admires on Tom. No, James is like a mangy dog just having been brought in from the streets and fed its first meal.

Perhaps she's being unkind. But she does know he's a lethal killer. He practically developed the agent protocols for NANA. He wrote the rulebook on Theta Techniques and Terminations of the same name, the processes and the techniques used by NINJAs for eradicating targets in dreamscape. You won't find these books at your local bookstore; you won't find them anywhere actually. There were only seven ever printed, and some years ago Claude decided to shred them all. All the strategies are now strictly taught through the oral tradition.

Claude is watching through the mirror. Like a steely-eyed hawk watching over his young, his gaze doesn't leave very often at all. His hands are folded over his chest, and Anthony stands on his left, a mirror image of Claude. To Claude's right is Yolanda. She is nervously chewing on her thumb. She just wants the whole episode behind them.

The clock's fingers are pinching out the last sixth of a pie. It is just past ten to three in the morning. Cold sweat is prickling at Tom's forehead as he races down Fifteenth Street toward Pennsylvania Avenue. He hopes he will make it in time. The president's life depends on it and perhaps even western democracy.

The last light ahead of him is red. Traffic is light, has been the whole way here. Tom slows down to a crawl. He wipes his head with his upper arm, looks both ways for traffic, and then carries on through the red light.

Up ahead a police car pulls out from around the corner, but the officer didn't see him run the red. Tom pulls up behind the police car and then pulls into a parking space on the side of the street. The cop keeps going south on Fifteenth Street, past Pennsylvania Avenue. Tom gives them a thirty second advantage and then pulls out of the parking spot and continues on down toward Pennsylvania Avenue.

A minute later, he turns west onto Pennsylvania Avenue and parks his car on the side, farthest away from the guard's box. Tom reaches into the back seat and grabs his light windbreaker. He puts it on with great discomfort and zips it partway up to hide as much of his wet abdomen as he can.

Tom gets out of the car and walks up to the guard in his box. Tom is smiling at the man, trying to look as non-confrontational as possible. Each step is an effort. It would have been easier to hobble along; the pain wouldn't have been as bad that way. But the last thing Tom wants is to give the guard something else to worry about other than the news he is about to share.

2:53 AM

Guard Post, White House, Washington, D.C.

A deep breath. Tom's smiling but it's not warming the ice on the guard's face. He's grim-looking, eyeing Tom cautiously as Tom walk toward him. Tom's got his hands out, palms up, showing him he's not armed. His left leg feels stiff with each step. He wants to grimace and grunt, but he can't. The guard steps out of his guard box and across his shoulders slings an M4. Tom's been seeing a lot of those lately. The muzzle isn't exactly aimed straight at him, but it's leaning that way.

"Stay right there," says the guard.

Tom stops in his tracks. He's about six feet away from the guard. The guy's dressed in military fatigues with a beret. He's young, maybe in his late twenties, clean shaven with a boyish face. It would be hard to take him seriously without his carbine. But the carbine doesn't have to say anything, and Tom's listening eagerly, like this is his first day at school. Tom puts his hands out farther from his body, still showing palms. He's taken to moving really slowly now, what with the guard's M4 muzzle making small circles in the air like a shark that's had a sniff of blood.

"White House is closed. No visitors. You best be getting on your way."

The guard is not far from his box. In fact, he could almost lean on it, he's that close.

"I know, sir," says Tom. "But I need you to listen to me for just a minute, please."

The guard waves the muzzle of the M4 up toward Tom's chest.

"I said the White House is closed and I don't have time to listen."

Tom doesn't move backward like the guard is hoping. The guard knows he can use lethal force on trespassers on the White House grounds, but this joker is barely on the grounds and he isn't really trespassing. The guard's training didn't exactly specify events like this.

"Listen carefully, please. I'm with an agency you've never heard of. NANA. It stands for National Agency of Nano Agents. We conduct super covert operations, assassinations really, and the president is in grave danger as we speak."

"Shit," thinks Tom, "no wonder Claude chose a name like NANA. Nobody's going to take it seriously and there's no way to verify the agency either. Clever bastard." Tom also doesn't have any ID that says he's a NANA agent. The only thing he's got that NINJAs get is a generic Army ID badge. He never thought about these kinds of things before. The secret spy stuff just seemed so cool, and serving his country, well, that was the idea. Now he can see the smarter aspects of Claude's dark genius. Or of having a super secretive spy agency that nobody knows about.

"Then I suppose you've got some ID to back that up."

Tom shakes his head wearily. "No sir, I don't. As I said, it's an agency you've never heard of, and nobody will verify it, but I do have Army ID. I'm just going to reach around into my back pocket for it now. Real slow."

The muzzle comes up and it's salivating at the spot on his chest where his heart is.

"Real slow, mister. Real slow."

Tom reaches around to both back pockets with his hands. He's moving like a snail frozen to a light pole. As slowly as he can. He doesn't like the look of the gaping maw of the carbine just begging to tunnel into his heart. He slips his left hand into his left back pocket, trying his hardest not to give away any indication of the pain at his side. The pocket is empty. He slips his right hand into his right back pocket. It's empty too. Shit, he just realizes that he left his Army ID at the motel he was staying at. He grits his teeth.

"Sorry, I just realized I left my ID at home."

The guard smirks. "Things are looking convenient all of a sudden for your story."

Tom brings his hands back out in front. Moving like he's been captured in slo-mo. "I know what you're thinking, soldier. Here's a guy at 3 AM who's come knocking at the White House with a crazy story, and none of his credentials can be verified. Am I right?"

The muzzle is still looking at him squarely in the chest. "You know I can use lethal force here, right?"

"I know that, soldier. Let me tell you a story. I've been with NANA for seven years. I'm thirty-eight. Before that I was with the CIA's Special Operations Group. You might have heard of them?"

The guard nods.

"Before that," Tom continues, "I was with DEVGRU for four years, and before that I was in the Navy. What I'm saying, soldier, is that I'm a ghost. The only thing you'll find out about me, Tomo Daisen, is that I was in the Navy when I got out of Naval Academy, which I joined in high school. After the Navy, your research will suggest that Tomo Daisen went into the private sector."

The guard drops the muzzle so it's looking at Tom's feet.

"Nobody's gonna wake the president at 3 AM just because some spook or lunatic says so."

Tom nods his head. "I know, but I've gotta try. Some agents have gone rogue and they're coming for the president."

"If you're ex-CIA, you know how secure the president is. Nobody's gonna get into the White House. The whole Chinese army couldn't get in."

"I know that. And this what I'm trying to tell you. We don't have to get in. We conduct assassinations via nanotechnology. You implant a little robot, tiny as a cell in someone's brain. Then when they go to sleep, you can kill them in their dreams and they die in real life. It looks natural, like a heart attack. I know it sounds crazy, but I'm telling you, they're coming for the president."

"It sounds like a fairytale. And I'm starting to think you're one of those crazy people that comes by here sometimes. I'm gonna have to ask you to leave before I arrest you for talking about assassinations and the president in the same breath, or worse, put a slug in you. Now, you seem like a nice guy, so I'm gonna pretend this never happened."

Tom shakes his head. "Listen, soldier. I am a nice guy. I'm one of the good guys, and I hoped it wasn't going to come to this. But I'm not going anywhere until you at least just make a phone call. Put a slug in me if you'd prefer. But there'll be a lot more paperwork for that choice then just making a phone call. And if I'm right, you'll be a hero to your country. Just think about it."

The guard looks at Tom for a while, and Tom holds his gaze steady. If push comes to shove, Tom is going to leave to fight another day. But maybe he can bluff his way into making the guy just make a phone call.

"All right, but nothing's gonna change. They're still not gonna wake the president 'cos I ask."

"At least we turn this situation into a win-win," says Tom, grinning.

"Stay right there."

The guard leans into his guard box and picks up a receiver and puts it to his ear. "Sergeant Mick Mackey."

There's a pause and the guard keeps his eye on Tom. Tom's not moving. He'll wait right where he is until they've come to some sort of closure.

"Sergeant, it's Corporal McTade....Yes, I'm sorry to disturb you, but I've got a guy out here who sounds convincing. He says he's ex-Navy, ex-CIA SOG....Yeah, I do actually believe him. He seems legit....No, no ID, but there's something about him seems familiar....Okay, well he says the president is in grave danger....I know, it sounds crazy....Yes sir, he says they can assassinate through some sort of technology, nanotechnology I think he said...." Tom nods at him. The guard keeps his eye on him. "That's right, sir. They don't need to be present to do it....Okay, I'll hold."

The guard looks at Tom. "They're not gonna wake him," he says.

"You never know," says Tom, still smiling. The pain is still his constant companion. He needs to get it looked at. He can feel the blood spreading across his lower abdomen, being absorbed by his t-shirt. It's starting to trickle its way down onto his boxer briefs. Tom hasn't lost a lot of blood, but the wound isn't going to close by itself, and he's starting to feel spacey.

"Yes sir, I'm still here....Interesting....Is that so?...So everything's good then....Yes, I understand. sorry to bother you, sir."

The guard hangs up the phone and looks at Tom. "As it happens, you got lucky. My sergeant put a call into the secret service. The president was up not long ago, rooting in the fridge for some milk. Apparently, he had a bad dream. Everything's fine."

Tom smiles. He managed to wake him up while he was in the dreamscape. But James will still go after him as soon as he gets back into REM.

"They'll still come after him as soon as he gets back to sleep," Tom says.

The guard is no longer looking friendly. "I'm done playing. I did what you asked. Now you've gotta leave."

"I will, but please, keep an eye out. Things will likely get darker before the dawn."

The guard waves his M4 up toward Tom's chest again. Tom doesn't like the look of it. "Everything's fine. I told you. Now go on home."

Tom slowly turns around and walks back toward his car. As he does so, the guard can see his bleeding through the opening of his jacket.

"Hey," says the guard. "You need a doctor?"

Tom stops and turns around just forty-five degrees. He looks at the guard over his shoulder.

"I'll take care of it myself. You've got bigger problems to worry about, soldier."

And Tom gets back into his car. He starts the engine and reverses back into oncoming traffic, but there is no traffic at this time of night. All he sees is a homeless man rolling a cart full of his belongings toward the guard's box. The homeless man stops and waits. He doesn't like the look of the rifle out in the open there. He waits until the guard steps back into his guard box and the homeless man crosses Pennsylvania Avenue.

Tom drives until he gets to the nearest gas station. He pulls out his phone and texts Margaret. He thinks he can trust her.

"Help, I need a doctor" is all his text says.

JASON BLACKER

2:57 AM

Run-Down Industrial Plant, Outside Washington, D.C.

Claude has never seen a man seem so relaxed in Theta for so long, doing nothing. He looks at his watch.

"Is this futile?" he mutters under his breath.

What Kathleen forgot to tell him when he had asked if James had entered Theta almost thirty minutes ago was if the president was in REM. Kathleen sure as hell is book smart, but sometimes she misses the obvious.

Like the fact that it takes not only the NINJA to be in Theta to eradicate his target, but also the target to be in REM. The president was not in REM. Tom somehow awakened him. In all the activity with Tom's quick departure, they didn't realize that the president also departed dreamscape.

James came out of Theta quickly and easily when he realized there was no place to go. However, Claude demanded he stay in Theta so that as soon as the president went back into REM, James could finish the task at hand.

"None of us are leaving until the task is completed," says Claude. He's been saying that a lot lately. Nobody is sure why he has to keep repeating himself. "I don't care if we have to wait until tomorrow morning; we're not leaving until this business has been taken care of."

"Can we at least take a toilet break?" asks Margaret.

Claude turns around and looks at her. "You need to go?"

She nods. Not really, but she wants to see if she can't get a hold of Tom on her cell phone.

"Okay, one at a time."

Claude escorts her to the door. He says to the soldier outside the door, "Escort her to the women's washroom and guard the door. If she doesn't come out in five minutes, and I mean five minutes exactly, you go in and haul out. I don't care if she's naked. Understood?"

The soldier with the bloody nose that has stopped bleeding nods. He follows Margaret down the hall to the washrooms. The men's and women's on this side are small. The women's washroom only has three stalls in it. There are no windows and there is only one way to enter and exit and that is by the same door.

Margaret smiles at the soldier. His face is smooth rock without emotion.

"I'll be much quicker than five minutes. Don't worry," Margaret says.

The soldier doesn't say anything. He watches her go in and he stands guard at the side of the door. Inside, the lights go on automatically, and Margaret looks under each of the three stalls to make sure there isn't anyone there. The chances are slim to none, and slim might be in the men's. Still, having worked for NANA since the beginning, paranoia slipped into her mind and made itself at home.

The washroom is empty and Margaret enters the stall. She sits down, fully clothed, and fishes into her pants pocket for her phone. She looks at it and realizes she hasn't yet turned it on. She does so and waits.

It seems to take an eternity for the phone to start. She's not wearing a watch, but if she were to guess, it's been three minutes since she entered the washroom when the home screen comes on. Margaret looks at the home screen. No service, it says.

"Shit," she thinks to herself. "I know that. I'm 150 feet underground and Claude doesn't want any means for electronic devices to capture and leak information out of here. At least, those electronic devices not deemed necessary for the task of R&D."

She can't reach Tom, and Tom can't reach her. He's alone out there. She hopes he made it, though a small part of her is wondering if he isn't lying dead just 150 feet above her head, having been shot down by the snipers as he tried to escape. She hurriedly waves the thoughts away. Tom's the best. If any NINJA could escape, it would be him.

Margaret gets off the toilet and flushes it. Nothing to flush, but she's got to keep up appearances. She thinks she's about four minutes in now. She powers off her phone to save battery for when she can get a signal. She turns on the tap and washes her hands. She doesn't pretend because, with her luck, Claude will want to smell them to make sure she actually cleaned up after herself. Not that he's ever done that. But the man is weird, and he's coming unglued tonight.

"Told you I'd be under five minutes," she says as she opens the washroom door.

The soldier looks at his watch. "You had seventeen seconds to spare," he says, all business.

"See, plenty of time."

Margaret steps back into the control room and Claude turns around and acknowledges her. He's wearing a big smile. The first real smile of the whole evening. Though it's really morning, it still feels like evening because Margaret hasn't gone to bed yet.

She walks up and stands behind Kathleen.

"How's things?" Margaret asks, trying to feign enthusiasm.

"Good, the president has just entered REM again."

It's been eleven months and eleven days since James last conducted an eradication. But it's like riding a bicycle. So easy to get back into the saddle, and the thrill is fresh once again. As a trainer, his focus is on training, not eradicating. But he's thrilled to be back in Theta theater again.

He likes to think he's still the best—after all, he wrote the book on it. And as much as Tom has been his finest student, in this case the student has not surpassed the teacher. Unlike Tom, James prefers to make his eradications quick and efficient. He's never understood Tom's preference for taking in the dreamscape and using what's at hand. No, James takes with him into the dreamscape a gun. This is how it should be, and perhaps if Tom had followed suggested protocols, they wouldn't be in this mess and General Bukhari would be dead already.

James enters the president's dreamscape. He looks around. He's sitting down in the Oval Office, and across from him is the president. He sees the blue beacon pulse in the president's head. Target has been identified. James has no scruples when it comes to his work. If this is in fact the president, then there's a good reason he's become a target and James will take him out. He will eradicate the threat like he's been trained to. Like he's trained others to do.

James looks down. He's dressed in a red dress and his fingernails are painted red. He's a woman, no doubt. But he does not have time for identifying the minutia in this dreamscape. He has identified the target and it's time to eradicate him.

"Prime Minister," the president says, "I want us to discuss how we might both benefit from the Japanese buying more of our bonds. As you know, the Chinese are losing their appetite for them, and besides, we prefer to help our friends who have helped us in return."

James smiles and nods. He stretches out his hand, and as he does so, a Glock 22 materializes in his hand and is aimed right at the president's forehead. James smiles, looking at the Glock in his hand. He knows Claude wouldn't approve—it's not American. But it's James's preferred handgun of choice and the one he personally owns at home. Besides, this isn't a real Glock in this dreamscape, and Claude will never know how he killed the president; or if James shares the how with him, he'll fib on the weapon used.

The president opens his mouth. Perhaps he is about to scream for help or he's just in shock. James isn't going to wait to find out. He pulls the trigger and the recoil feels real in his hand and the entry wound looks real. His work is done. In less than a couple of seconds, this dreamscape will evaporate around him and he'll come out of Theta.

James opens his eyes. He gets up onto his elbows and looks through the one-way mirror. All he can see is the reflection of his own head, dotted with the white scabs of electrodes.

"EOL?" he asks, grinning. He loves the action and the thrill. With Tom out of the picture, hopefully permanently, he'll get to be in the driver's seat more often.

"EOL confirmed," Kathleen responds over the speakers.

James lies back down, savoring the win, the victory. It feels good. And if indeed it was the president of the United States that he just now assassinated, that'll be one for the history books. He never liked the president anyway.

"Don't get too comfortable," says Claude over the speakers. "You still have to deal with General Bukhari."

"I can't wait," says James.

James closes his eyes and folds his hands over his belly. He feels serene and calm, like a Zen master. This is why he loves this job. You can change the world from the comfort of your bed. No need to get up and personal and bloody anymore.

6:17 AM

Elkins, West Virginia

Not far from the Federal Building on Henry Avenue, there's a little diner that Tom has crawled into and found his way into a booth. The place is mostly empty. A couple of truckers are up at the bar eating big plates of greasy food. An older couple is up early having a leisurely breakfast. And one other guy has his head resting on his forearm which is on the table. He looks like a student coming off a bender.

Just over a couple of hours ago, before he left Washington, Tom left his car at the motel he has been at ever since arriving in Washington. He sanitized it as best he could. He had a sponge bath and changed his clothes. He also changed cars. He took some guy's old Buick that must've been twenty years old. Nothing more than a rust bucket, and he left him his Camaro. The guy got a deal. Wouldn't cost much to fix up some bullet holes.

And that's why he left it. Cops have a keen eye for pulling folks over with bullet holes in the sides of their cars.

His gunshot wound is still leaking blood. It feels hot and he is starting to feel like he has a fever. He knows that isn't a good sign.

If he doesn't hear from Margaret soon, he'll have to find a doctor himself, and the only friend he has within three hundred miles of this place is a high school buddy in Cincinnati who he hasn't seen in years. He also has some family up in New York City, but heading there would be asking for trouble. He also isn't a doctor, and the last he knew, Tom was in the Navy.

"What can I get ya, hon?"

The waitress took her time getting here. That's how they move in these parts sometimes. Tom has been in this little diner around five minutes already. On the table in front of him is a napkin dispenser and salt and pepper shakers with a menu sandwiched between them. Tom hasn't looked at the menu.

"Coffee and toast."

"Anything else?"

The waitress looks down at him. She might have been attractive once, when she was knee-high to a grasshopper. Now, it looks like time has taken a blade to her face and slashed it wantonly. Her hair is store-bought rust-dyed that needs some fixing. The roots are a half-inch of grey. She smells of cigarettes and cheap perfume.

Tom looks up at her and smiles, keeping the brim of his baseball cap down low over his eyes.

"That's all, thanks."

The waitress yawns as she turns away and walks back to the kitchen. Tom bought the baseball cap and a pair of purple John Lennon sunglasses at a Walmart on his way out of Washington. He also bought bandages, which were wrapped snugly across his stomach. They are helping staunch the blood, but what he needs is a doctor.

The food comes quicker than Tom thought it would. A serving of toast is four half pieces. He is grateful for that. She plunks down a holder of small jams and peanut butter. His choices are grape jelly, strawberry jam, marmalade, and peanut butter. One of each for his halves of toast, and that's what he decides to do with them.

She also fills a cup she brings with coffee and dribbles some on the table in front of him. She stifles another yawn.

"Can I get you anything else, hon? My shift is finishing up here," she says, looking at her watch.

"How much do I owe you?"

She's come prepared. She drops down his bill. He owes five and a quarter. Tom pulls out some bills from his right pocket, wincing as he does so. He peels off a ten and puts it down.

"Keep the change," he says.

"Thanks, hon," she says and leaves, heading over to the older couple to top off their coffee. The old man puts his hand over his cup; the wife takes a refill. Tom's phone vibrates. He fishes it out of his jacket.

"You're on TV. I'm glad you're okay."

It's from Margaret. He looks up and scans the room. Just behind the counter to the right of the cash register, angled toward him, he can see a TV. It's small and the volume is low. He can't hear it. A TV anchor is talking, but he doesn't know what she's saying. But then there's a picture of the president. Underneath the caption reads, "President Towles assassinated." Then they cut to a picture of him. It's not the best picture, probably taken by the soldier in the guard box he spoke with. "Tomo Daisen," the caption underneath his picture says, "wanted in the murder of President Towles. Considered armed and dangerous."

Then they cut to a live video of Vice President Veronica Matney. Tom looks back down to his vibrating phone. "Shit," he thinks. They shouldn't know it's an assassination, except he's opened up his big mouth about how the president was in danger and they were going to try and kill him. Now it looks like he's gone rogue. They'll put it all on him, and NANA, Claude, and the rest of them will be off the hook.

He gets another text from Margaret. "Go to 6725 Verona Rd Penn Hills PA. Ask for Doc Miller, Joshua. He'll help."

Tom takes a piece of toast and shoves half of it in his mouth. He takes a swirl of coffee and looks up at the TV. The two truckers are still at the counter, minding their food, not looking at the TV. Tom starts typing on his phone.

"Thanks. I'll contact you later. Erase and lose the phone."

He looks back at her last text and burns the address to memory. Then he erases all messages, sent, and trashed. He takes the SIM card out of his phone as well as the battery. He shoves the other half of the piece of toast in his mouth, leaving two halves untouched on the plate. He takes a last swig of coffee, and stands up gingerly. As he does he sees a cop walk into the diner, looking around. Tom turns away from the door and heads toward the bathroom at the back, trying not to limp.

As he does he hears, "Ten thirty-five, Tomo Daisen, Japanese-American, armed and dangerous..." Tom can't hear the rest. The cop has turned his radio down. He swallows hard, the realization of how much trouble he's in, just for trying to do the right thing, is dawning on him, just like this day.

Every cop in the nation will be making Tomo their sole focus. Hell, Interpol is going to make this a priority. You don't assassinate the leader of the free world and expect to walk away from it. But Tom's gotta find some proof before he gives himself up. NANA is going to stack the deck against him.

Tom heads into the washroom, wondering what to do. If he knows cops, and he does, the guy's gonna take a seat facing the door so he can keep an eye on the comings and goings. He needs a Hail Mary. He looks at himself in the mirror and splashes cold water on his face. He takes out his phone and the battery. He wraps them each separately in paper towels and makes sure to toss them into the bottom of the trashcan. He doesn't want to make it any easier for them to find him. He knows they can find him via the nanos in his body, and he curses, wondering how the hell he ever thought it was a good idea to get them implanted. Then he remembers. He needs them to carry out his assassinations. Anyway, not any Tom, Dick, and cop can access his nanos like they can his cell phone. You need specialized equipment, and as far as he knows, only NANA has that. A few minutes go by. He's gotta try and leave. He'll have to take his chances.

Outside, Tom hears sirens. Could it be the Hail Mary he's hoping for? Tom slowly walks out of the bathroom and hovers around the hallway. Diagonally across, he has a view of the parking lot outside the diner. The cop is in his car, peeling out around the corner, lights and sirens blaring, called away for some reason. Tom will take it.

He walks out of the diner, head down, and gets into his car. There's only one stop he needs to make before he heads for Penn Hills. Tom starts up the old Buick, hot-wiring it like he did the first time. Nobody's watching him, so him leaning in down by the steering wheel doesn't look to out of place.

Tom drives away from the diner, carefully and well within the law. He signals at every turn and doesn't exceed the speed limit. At every stop sign, he comes to a complete stop. He drives up and down a few of the quieter residential roads here in Elkins and down a couple of alleys. Finally, he likes what he sees.

He pulls his car up next to a white Taurus, probably at least ten years old. Tom stalls the Buick and wipes it down as best he can. He looks around. It's light now, but this neighborhood is quiet. All he can hear is a dog barking now and then. Tom gets out of the Buick, wipes it down again, and closes the door. He wipes the door down again too.

He tries the driver's door of the Taurus. What he loves about small towns is the carefreeness they still offer. The trust in humanity. He's about to punish that trust, but it can't be helped. The door is unlocked and Tom slips in, quiet as a mouse, closing it ever so softly. In a few minutes, he's on the 33 heading west in his brand new set of wheels. His fever's getting hotter, and the wound is burning like someone's stuck him with a cigarette.

11:03 AM

Run-Down Industrial Plant, Outside Washington, D.C.

At just after 6 AM, Claude let Anthony, Yolanda, and Margaret go for the day, though he wanted them to report back in at noon. It is getting closer to noon than he'd like and the fucking Iranian has still not entered REM. Claude can almost taste it. He can imagine General Bukhari falling asleep right before his eyes. The Iranians somehow managed to keep him up all this time, but eventually he'll have to sleep. And when he goes to sleep, NANA will be waiting for him.

At 4:00 this morning, when it remained apparent that the target was not going to enter REM anytime soon, Claude allowed James to get some rest. James slept like a baby until around ten, when he awoke with his game face on, ready to take care of business.

That's what Claude likes about James, and the reason he chose him as the first NINJA. He is reliable and trustworthy. A soldier who knows his place and doesn't question orders. If he only had more like James, NANA wouldn't have gotten into this mess in the first place. But Claude knows how difficult it was to find men who can do the work of a NANA NINJA. Many are chosen but few finish the training.

Tom was ideal. Top of his class at the Naval Academy, shit, now that Claude thinks about it, Tom was top of his group at everything he did. The only thing he'd known since high school was the military, and yet he grew a conscience, took a critical view, started examining things. That was uncalled for. Claude is a good man, a true patriot. The president wasn't. It's not like Claude was trying to overthrow the government. He's just trying to make America better, move someone else into power who understands the stakes like he does.

But Tom had to end up as a fly in the ointment. If he wasn't found by the end of the day today, he'd have to take him out personally. Well, not him; James. Though that worries Claude. As much as James was his original NINJA, and as much as James might protest, Claude feels that Tom is better at dreamscape assassination. Hell, Tom is better at everything. And Tom has to enter REM sleep at some point, and when he does, the element of surprise was with NANA, not with Tom.

James walks into the control room, coming back from the washroom.

"Any word yet?" he asks.

Claude shakes his head.

"No," says Kathleen, "I can't quite explain it, but he's got to enter REM soon. He's been asleep for about twenty minutes."

Kathleen's watching the computer with a furrowed brow. She's finding this whole event stressful. She's glad for the money, but she thought she would have been finished hours ago. And yet, here she is in the middle of a new day. And she doesn't like the tone in Claude's voice. She's not happy to be involved in the president's assassination, though she still can't quite believe that's what happened.

She feels like she's stuck between a rock and a hard place. This was supposed to be a good job. Developing cutting-edge nano technology that could help people, create a better world. That's what she was promised, but instead her work has been twisted into military use. She knew that from the beginning, but it seems like she's been hoodwinked and ended up in some sort of nightmare.

And now she's paid for this dance and she'll have to hold onto the devil 'til it's done. She sighs, exhaling at her bangs. Claude looks down at her.

"This will all be over soon," he says. "I'm grateful that you're seeing things through. It's important. And I know that right now, you might not be able to see the good in what we've been doing, but trust me, we're doing God's work. This is for the good of the American people. Hell, it's for the betterment of humankind."

Kathleen looks up at him shyly and tries to smile, but it's feeble and wobbly and doesn't last long.

"I'm just glad to be back in the saddle," grins James.

The computer holographic image beeps and draws their attention to it.

"We have REM," says Kathleen excitedly. She excited if only because it means she might be getting home soon now. She's on the homestretch.

"Okay, quickly. Let's get to it," says Claude.

Kathleen and James enter the Theta room. James strips down to his boxers and lies down. Kathleen attaches the electrodes back to his head and upper chest and upper arms. She is slower at this than Margaret is. She feels like she's all thumbs.

"Okay, give me one sec," she says as she hurries back into the control room.

Inside the control room, she taps away at the keyboard, verifying she's got a sync with James's nano.

"Okay, James, good to go."

Claude sits down beside her and he watches as she watches. She taps away at the keyboard occasionally. They're looking for confirmation that James has entered dreamscape. It doesn't take long. Three minutes at the most. The computer beeps again, and on the holographic screen in front of them the image changes color and glows for a brief moment. Claude doesn't understand all of this.

"What does that mean?" he asks.

"It means we're in. James has entered the target's dreamscape."

Claude smiles. This long night and morning is now finally paying off. He can smell the victory in his grasp. One last loose end to finish up after this.

Jaleh is nodding off in the chair beside her mother. It's not very comfortable, but the intermittent beeping of the machines attached to her father is soothing, and her father's snoring is rhythmical. It didn't take her father long to fall asleep, and Usama suggested they try and rest. It would be a long night, as they had many tests to conduct when her father reawakened.

But something seems wrong. Jaleh shifts her position but she can't fall back asleep. She is becoming more and more awake as the seconds ticked by. Something is different. She opens her eyes quickly in a panic, her heart beating like a horse around a track. "What is wrong?" she thinks. "Something seems wrong."

Then it dawns on her. The machines stopped beeping. The heart rate monitor was a straight line. A dead line. And then it starts on with a constant beep.

"Father!" she yells, jumping up and running over to him. She grabs at his shoulders and shakes him.

"Father!" she yells again.

Soraya is now up and she has come over to the side of the bed. "What's wrong?" Panic is thick and clogging up her voice.

"Call the nurses, get the doctors, Daddy's heart has stopped!"

Soraya looks at her husband and then at her daughter, then at the machine, and she sees the straight line. She understands it. Jaleh starts chest compressions as her mother runs out the door to call the nurses.

It isn't long, perhaps a minute, before the nurses and the emergency doctor on call come rushing in. They take over from Jaleh. She gives them room, and she and her mother huddle, watching the action as the emergency medical team try drugs, defibrillation, and oxygen. After fifteen minutes, the doctor pronounces General Armin Bukhari dead. He turns to them.

"I'm sorry," he says. "There is nothing we can do."

Soraya falls to the floor, clutching at her hair, and she starts to wail. Jaleh squats down to comfort her mother as the nurses cover Armin's body with a sheet. Baraz bursts into the room and stops just inside the door.

"What's going on?" he asks loudly as he comes up to his sister and mother.

Jaleh stands up and wipes the tears from her eyes. "Those American bastards," she says, crying again, the words tumbling and breaking as they come out. "The Americans killed Daddy."

JASON BLACKER

11:11 AM
Penn Hills, Pittsburgh

Tom has been on the road for over four and a half hours. That means he's changed cars four times already. He started out with the white Taurus, thanks to the kind folks in Elkins. Next up, he got an old Datsun 710 two-door pickup truck in Grafton, West Virginia. At this stage, beggars couldn't be choosers. It was a rust bucket, really, that he didn't think you could still find anywhere. It had a small four-cylinder engine, which wined and moaned and cried all along the highway, barely making it over sixty-five miles an hour.

In Morgantown, he ditched the Datsun, smiling ironically at how Claude would never have approved of him driving around in a foreign automobile, let alone a truck. He picked up a '96 Chevy Impala at the far end of a Walmart parking lot. It was a burgundy brown and a hell of a lot of fun to drive. In fact, he almost got pulled over by the state patrol except for the fact they'd been busy with another driver. He must have been coming up on them at a hundred miles an hour, slowing quickly when he saw them.

In Uniontown, Pennsylvania, Tom changed out his Impala for a green '66 Volkswagen Kombi, his second ride this trip that Claude would have frowned at. He smiled at that again, but that made his side ache, and it wasn't really that funny. They were probably hunting him down right at this very point.

He remembered in high school taking a road trip with one of his mates in a VW van much like the one he picked up in Uniontown. It was a spring break trip to San Francisco. But riding in a van from Uniontown up to Pittsburgh caught a few eyes. It wasn't his smartest move. Maybe he chose it because of nostalgia, though he liked to think he chose the van because it was easier to hotwire.

He ditches the van in the suburbs of Pittsburgh, choosing more carefully his last ride into Penn Hills. It is a white Ford Focus, two-door hatchback, probably a 2000 model. He saw plenty of them on his drive up here, so it won't stick out like a sore thumb. More than that, this one looks it hasn't been driven in a few weeks at least. It has a soft layer of tawny dust on it and it has trouble starting. But once he gets it up and going it purrs right along.

He found this one in another Walmart parking lot. Walmart has been good to him on this trip. He also stopped in at this particular Walmart and bought a disposable smartphone. He prepaid for a gig of data and one hundred minutes of talk and one hundred texts. He figures that will be plenty. Tom isn't going to be sticking around the US for very long. He has to get out in order to save himself and figure out how to bring NANA down for what they did.

Tom drives away from the Walmart, and just a few minutes out, he pulls to the side of the road. He opens up his phone and turns it on. He needs to find out what is going on with him on the news. It is coming on quarter to eleven by this point and the "manhunt" for the president's killer, as they put it, has Tom in somewhere in Washington. There is video of his beloved Camaro parked outside the motel and the camera crew is interviewing the guy whose Buick he bartered his Camaro for.

The guy is bellyaching about how his beloved Buick was stolen. Thing is, he probably couldn't have gotten a thousand bucks for that rust bucket Tom managed to caress all the way to Elkins.

He is an old fat man with gray hair all brushed back. Saying how he woke up to find his car gone and this bullet-riddled Camaro in the parking lot not far away. Then he says he decided to call the cops. You can tell he's really proud of himself. He's smiling as he looks around at all the cops crawling around in the parking lot, peering into the Camaro. He figures he's a real hero, helping to capture America's most wanted murderer.

In the background, the police are opening up the trunk and they pull out the M4. The cameraman is quick on this and zooms in, probably gesturing to the reporter as she turns around and starts talking about what the police have found. But Tom cancels out of that video and looks for another one. He finds what he wants on CNN.

What Tom wants to know above all else is where they think he's headed. He starts the video. The anchor woman is going on about how they've found his Camaro. He fast-forwards to the part he wants and listens.

"As we've mentioned this before, Tomo Daisen is considered armed and dangerous. He is a highly decorated combat veteran and has been involved in the highest levels of top-secret service to his country. If you see him, call police. Do not—and we can't stress this enough—do not try and engage him personally."

On the anchor woman's left side is a picture of Tom as she continues speaking. "We believe that Tomo Daisen, who also goes by Tom, is headed out west toward Cincinnati where he has contacts, or he might be trying to make his way home to San Bernardino. Police are also advising you to be on the lookout for anyone matching Daisen's description heading into New York City where he has family."

The anchor woman then goes on about how to contact police with any information, that they've set up a special hotline, etcetera. Tom breathes a sigh of relief. At least they arern't expecting him in this part of the northeast.

Tom makes his way up to Penn Hills. He drives down Verona Road. It is a sleepy community where folks mind their own business. Where you could raise a family, living the American dream while the rest of the country fights tooth and nail for scraps and glimmers of hope, like his folks did in San Bernan. He drives around the block a few times before stopping fifty feet from 6725. He doesn't know this guy, doesn't know if he can trust him. But the last time he checked his wound around thirty minutes ago, it was looking ugly. It was firm to the touch and hot, and it had started oozing puss. His temperature felt higher too.

Tom drives up and turns into the driveway. He looks at the house. It is well-kept, large with nice grounds. He parks under the shade of a large tree. He opens the door and climbs out, wincing at the pain. He closes the door softly and stands for a moment by the car. It is quiet here; he can't hear anything. The rustling of leaves in the trees and a birdcall now and then. No traffic, no children out playing, but it is a school day. He looks around. No nosy neighbors, no dogs barking either. It is almost too quiet for all of Tom's training.

He can't see any cars in the driveway. Perhaps they are in the garage, or, knowing his luck, perhaps Doctor Miller isn't home. Then he'll be screwed. Tom walks up to the door and knocks. He knocks loudly five or six times. He needs help. He needs for the guy to be home.

11:15 AM

Penn Hills, Pittsburgh

For a while, nothing happens. Tom stands and listens to the whistling trees and the chirping birds. He's feeling a little light-headed and shaky. He hasn't eating anything for a long time. Well, other than that measly piece of toast and cup of coffee. Not enough to keep his strength up. But he's not convinced that it's just the lack of food that's making him feel weak.

He lifts his hand again to give it one more try. He'll knock one more time, and if nobody answers then he'll head to a clinic and play the cards he's been dealt. His hand is up ready to strike at the stubborn door when it opens.

A big man, likely in his seventies, is in gray slacks and a white shirt with thin blue stripes on it running vertically. His gray slacks are held up by red suspenders. Tom looks up at him, he looks like the spitting image of Churchill. He's also got an unlit stogie in the corner of his mouth. Tom figures he's gotta be around six six; he's stocky, with just a soft padding of pudding over his muscles. If he were steak he'd be marbled. His thin gray wisps of hair are combed backward, and his eyebrows are bushy slugs across his eyes. He looks grumpy, until he starts to smile and it transforms his face. His eyes twinkle.

"Tom, you must be Tom," he says, and his voice comes across like thunder hidden deep inside his belly. "Maggie told me to expect you."

Tom's leaning on the doorframe. Things are starting to feel surreal now. He's not sure if he can take any more steps. Tom tries to smile and he offers his hand. Doctor Miller swallows it whole in one of his and tries to yank it loose from the wrist. Then he gives it back. Tom's surprised it's still attached to his arm.

"I'm Josh Miller, but my friends call me Doc. Call me Doc."

Doc's right arm is circling behind Tom as he invites him in. Tom steps forward and loses consciousness. Doc grabs him under his armpits and closes the door with his foot. He carries Tom to the back of the house to a guestroom where he lays him on the bed. Doc's felt the 1911 tucked in the back of Tom's pants. He takes it out and places it on the side table. Tom starts to regain consciousness.

He sees Doc looking down at him. His windbreaker is off and his t-shirt is up around his chest. Doc is peeling back the dressings Tom had put over his wound.

"How do you feel, son?"

Tom looks up at Doc. Doc's face is crinkled into a smile and he has a way about him that calms Tom. The best term he can up with to describe Doc is grandfatherly, in all the best ways.

"I've felt better, Doc."

Doc nods. He's still biting onto his unlit cigar. He peels the rest of the bandages off and takes a look at the wound. It's messy with wet and dried blood and oozing puss. It smells like the beginning of rancidity is starting to set in.

"I'm going to poke around a bit, might hurt a bit. Tell me when it hurts a lot."

Doc starts poking around the edges of the wound, working outward. Tom's face is tight ball of wincing pain.

"Any pain?" asks Doc, looking at the wound.

"A lot of pain, everywhere."

"You arrived just in time, son," says Doc. "This wound is starting to go bad. Doesn't look like it hit vitals or main vessels— you're lucky. Then again, I doubt you would've got here if it had."

Tom nods. "I felt pretty good until just now."

"That's adrenaline for you, son. You've been living off adrenaline I daresay since you got shot. When was that?"

Tom shrugs. "Around two, two thirty, I think."

Doc frowns and puts his mouth upside down. "That's a long time without medical help," he says. "Wait here. I'm going to get my kit."

Doc pats Tom on the shin, smiles at him, and gets up and walks out the room. Tom looks around. His heart is beating like a wobbly spinning top in his chest. The room is soft blues. There's a side table with his gun on it. His jacket is down by his feet. On his right side on the far wall is a dresser. Above it is a framed poster of Schweitzer with a caption that reads, "Think occasionally of the suffering of which you spare yourself the sight."

The curtains are a pale yellow and are drawn open. The bright daylight is filling the room to bursting but it isn't direct. Tom still feels the cool stillness of the room's air on his exposed stomach.

Doc comes back into the room, carrying a large plastic box with many drawers in it in his one hand. His other is throttling an IV stand that he carries over and puts next to the side table.

"I'm going to give you an IV with fluids, electrolytes, and I'm going to have to give you intravenous antibiotics if we're to fix you up quickly and put a stop to the infection."

Tom nods. "I like your poster and quote up there," he says looking at Schweitzer.

Doc looks over at it and smiles. "It's a good reminder of why I got into this business of medicine. It also helps remind me of why I've made other choices along the way."

Doc takes a look at Toms arms, he's so lean that his veins are like tubes wrapped around his wrists. He won't need a tourniquet to find a vein. Then Doc looks at the wound again.

"You were shot from behind, correct?"

Tom nods. "Yes I was."

"Okay, lets get you on your stomach so I can knit you back together before I give you the IV."

Tom struggles to turn over, wincing, with the help of Doc.

"What other things does the poster remind you of?" asks Tom.

Doc looks back at it and smiles, thinking about Schweitzer and his dynasty of care and compassion that he extended toward the circle of life, not just humanity.

"Well," says Doc, "Schweitzer's philosophy of Reverence for Life affected me, and like him, I became vegetarian many years ago as a natural extension of that philosophy."

"I was raised vegetarian too," says Tom, his head turned facing toward the dresser. "My parents raised me as a Buddhist, and part of that included a vegetarian diet."

Doc reaches into his bag and pulls out a syringe and needle and a small bottle of liquid. "I'm going to give you a couple of injections of anesthetic," he says.

Tom doesn't say anything. Doc fills the syringe with some of the liquid. He pinches a piece of Tom's back, hard enough that Tom can feel it and then he inserts the needle. It's a trick Doc learned from a colleague years ago. You create an uncomfortable sensation close to the injection point, and the needle is barely felt at all.

"Are you still?" asks Doc, finishing the injection.

"What? Buddhist or vegetarian?"

"Both."

"I'd say I'm a non-practicing Buddhist—hard to be a practicing Buddhist in my line of work. And I'm vegetarian, but I wasn't always. I went through a rebellious period."

Doc nods his head. "Tell me if you can feel this." He pokes and pinches around the wound.

"Just a little," says Tom.

Doc takes out some alcohol wipes and cleans the wound thoroughly. "Now?"

"Nothing," says Tom.

Doc goes to work stitching Tom up. It doesn't take long. Then he cleans the wound again and applies a topical antibiotic before taping a gauze dressing over the wound.

"Okay, that wasn't too bad was it? We can put you on your back now."

"Didn't feel a thing, Doc. You've got soft hands."

Doc smiles as he helps Tom back onto his back.

"More doctors could do well to practice soft hands. I reckon that half or more of the pain a patient feels coming out of anesthetic is caused by doctors not treating the surgery with soft, gentle hands. If you could see how they physically manipulate the body during surgery; it's butchery. You'd be shocked. For what should be an art of finesse, they take too little care in tenderness."

Doc reaches into his bag again and pulls out an IV bag and hangs it on the IV stand. He reaches back in and pulls out a smaller bag which is the antibiotics and attaches that to the IV stand too. He puts the cannula from the antibiotic's bag into the injection port. He pushes the needle into Tom's wrist and taps it down. Then he adjusts the clamp.

"This'll probably feel warm," Doc says, and it does. "It should also start making you feel better in a few minutes."

Doc starts cleaning the front side of Tom's gunshot wound. "What kind of work are you in, Tom?"

Tom looks down at Doc, watching him clean his wound and then inject him with a local anesthetic. He's not sure if he should tell him, though he figures he might as well. Otherwise he'll just get his information from the news which is fabricated and full of lies.

"You've probably seen what they're saying about me on the news by now."

Doc nods as he recleans the wound, giving the anesthetic time to work. "I don't pay much attention to the news. To bastardize Twain, there are three kinds of lies. Lies, damn lies, and the news."

Tom laughs and then stops; it hurts too much. "You've got that right."

Doc starts suturing the wound.

"I work for a government agency that you've never heard of, and never will. It's called NANA. National Agency of Nano Agents. A cute name for what is a very lethal agency. We kill people in their sleep, from afar."

Doc stops the suturing and looks up at Tom, raising his eyebrows.

"Honestly, Doc, that's what I do. This agency has developed little nano robots that I'm riddled with, and we deliver them into our target, and through meditation, basically, once the target is in REM sleep, I enter their dreams and kill them. Killing them in their dreams sends a trigger to the nanobot inside them which stops their heart through an electrical and/or chemical response. It's easy, and we can never be found out. It looks like a natural death."

Doc finishes up stitching the front of the wound. He looks up at Tom again. "That sounds like science fiction, horrific science fiction."

"I know," says Tom, putting his left hand under his head. "But it's the way we operate, and they wanted me to kill the president. I couldn't do that, so I left, got shot leaving, and they probably had my mentor do the assassination and now they're putting it on me."

"And they'll be coming for you as soon as they can I bet."

Tom nods his head wearily. "Yeah, but the worst part is they don't actually have to be here to kill me. They can just connect their nanobot with mine, and when I fall asleep they'll have at me."

"How can I help, son?"

"Well, when you're finished up here, if you could get me a whole roll of aluminum foil, I might be able to make it thick enough to create a helmet to block the signals. The problem with that is that it requires all the nanos to be in my head, which they should be as a NINJA, but if they can't receive any signals for a while they'll start travelling to my extremities looking for a signal. In the meantime, it'll buy me time to figure out my next move. And I'll try and get some sleep once I'm wearing my tinfoil hat."

Doc grins and finishes up dressing the wound and covers it up with Tom's t-shirt. "I think you need sleep. I'll go and get some aluminum foil and let you rest. Then we'll need to come up with a plan to get you someplace safe. How much time will it buy you?"

"I'm not sure. Training suggested that nanos only look for a signal every three hours if they're dormant. If they can't find a signal after two cycles or six hours, some nanos will work their way toward my extremities. Doesn't take them longer than a few minutes to get into place. Then if after another two cycles, or another six hours, they still can't find a signal, they'll start beaming a signal of their own ever fifteen minutes. They take so long because we're seldom out in the field without a support team, and most of the nanotechnology is used for linking up and the signal strength used for assassination. The linking up is all passive, conducted by much larger hardware."

"Doesn't seem like a long time to me," says Doc as he gets up to leave.

JASON BLACKER

11:33 AM

Run-Down Industrial Plant, Outside Washington, D.C.

For the last few minutes they've all been congratulating each other on a job well done. Mostly they've been congratulating James, who did a terrific job of eradicating two threats in one night. He now ties the record with Tom, who couldn't manage three. And if he had, they wouldn't be in this mess now anyway. No other NINJA has attempted two because it's against protocol, but Claude is flexible when it comes to what he wants, and he wanted the Iranian and the president dead in the same night. And he got his wish.

"Well done, James," says Claude, shaking his hand. "We should have had you as our NINJA all along."

Claude is grinning now. Gone is his sour face and angry tones. He feels like a huge weight has been shifted off his chest. But there is one other loose end that he needs to finish up, and then the world will be right side up again.

Kathleen is all grins. She's glad this night, this ordeal really, is behind her. She feels like they've made it through a minefield and dodged a ton of bullets. Now NANA is safe, as is her job. So long as Claude doesn't head off the deep end again like he's done on this occasion. She can sit and watch while one president is assassinated, but she won't do it for a second one.

She doesn't like her future in NANA with an unstable Claude at the helm. She's always found him driven and perhaps overzealous in his patriotism, but up until this point his decisions have all been sound. Kathleen somehow fell into this debacle and she'll need to figure out a defense if it comes to that. She can't plea insanity, but she can fudge her knowledge. Claude never told them they were assassinating the president; in fact he downright denied it. Therefore, she never knew whom they were eradicating. If she had known, by God, she'll say, she would have left and tried her luck with the snipers.

That's a good defense, and it's true, except for the part that as the lead scientist she knows you can't reimage the target's avatar in dreamscape. Still, there are only two other scientists in this organization who know that—Daniel Chadbourne and Jose Rivera—and neither of them were here tonight.

Kathleen sighs a breath of relief and smiles a small, genuine smile at Claude.

"I think this deserves a small celebration," he says. "Kathleen, would you do the honors."

A few months ago, Claude brought in a bottle of bubbly and had Kathleen store it in the small bar fridge in her office. She has since then bought six champagne flutes for enjoying it. A $3,000 bottle of champagne had to be drunk from a real glass flute, not a plastic beer mug which were the only kinds of cups she could locate here before she bought the flutes.

Claude walks her out of the control room. He watches her walk down the hall toward her office.

"Everyone is free to go now. You are all dismissed. Thank you for your service," Claude says to the soldiers standing guard outside the control room.

"Yes sir," they say in unison, saluting and then dismissing themselves after a long shift.

Claude doesn't have to wait long for Kathleen to return. He holds the door open for her and they walk inside. She only brings half the flutes, as that's all that's needed. Claude opens the bottle of 2008 Krug Clos d'Ambonnay gently. This is not a bottle of frat champagne you shake around and shake all over each other. Each mouthful is to be enjoyed and savored.

Kathleen holds out a flute and Claude pours it half full. She hands this one to James. The next one she keeps for herself and the third is for Claude. Claude raises his hand with the flute in it.

"Here's to America, our beloved. May we live at her bosom all our years and die in her lap without any fears."

"Hear, hear," says Kathleen.

"I'll drink to that," says James.

Claude adds, "And may NANA continue valiant, true and strong, be her shield and sword all our days long."

Claude takes a long sip and the others too.

"Good champagne," says James.

Kathleen nods in agreement.

"For three grand a bottle, I should hope so," says Claude.

"What were you saving it for?" asks Kathleen.

"A celebration, like today's. Nothing specific."

They all sit down around the table, exhausted but thrilled, adrenaline still winding its way through their veins like electricity. Claude looks at James and Kathleen in turn.

"I know it's been a long and difficult night. But you will not go unrewarded. I have decided to give you both a bonus of $100,000 each."

James grins. "Thank you."

He's just excited to have gotten back into the saddle. He would have done it for free, though he appreciates the financial reward. Killing presidents after all, does carry with it a certain risk.

Kathleen nods. "Thanks Claude," she says. "So this is blood money," she thinks. She never imagined she'd be paid blood money. But it'll help assuage her guilt and pay for a lawyer if she's left out to dry. She doesn't think that'll happen, but the sour taste in her mouth over this event has not yet fully dissipated. And so long as this is the last of this kind of unauthorized assassination against an American, she figures she can learn to deal with it.

Claude looks at them and smiles. Some people, like himself, are true patriots. They don't need financial reward in order to do the right thing. In fact, it is their pleasure and their honor to serve their country. Claude thinks that James is one of those men, though the true color of his patriotism will only come to light in time.

Kathleen on the other hand is a patriot of convenience. Not one of the few willing to make the necessary sacrifices in the trenches for the good of her country. Still, like Judas, these people can be made to journey along the road of patriotism if the price is right. Claude, if he's good at one thing, is judging character. Six figures is a small price to pay to steer Kathleen down this road of true patriotism. Still, he will need to keep a close eye on her.

"Listen," he says, "before we go, there is one thing I need to find out. Give me a moment."

Claude gets up and goes over to the far side of the control room and picks up a telephone.

"Hi, Ty," he says. "It's been a long trying night. Sorry I haven't been touch sooner. Can you fill me on the events of earlier this morning."

There's a long pause.

"Uh huh....Okay....Really? All right, thanks for your help. I'll be up shortly."

Claude turns around and his face is a poker mask. Neither James nor Kathleen can determine whether the news is good or bad. Claude comes back and sits down.

"Kathleen, can you find out where Tom is?"

James looks at him and furrows his brow. "You mean he's not dead? He made it through those snipers upstairs."

Claude nods. "He took out two of our men before escaping, but they seem to think they wounded him on the way out. They've notified all hospitals in a two-hundred-mile radius. They think he's either headed to New York where he has family or to Cincinnati where he has a contact. My bet is on New York."

Kathleen puts her flute down. It's almost empty, one sip left. She starts tapping away at the keyboard. In a few moments, a holographic image appears from the middle of the table.

"What's his agent number?" asks Kathleen.

"NN 003."

"I thought so," says Kathleen.

NN 001 is sitting in front of her in this room. That's James Seaton. 002 was Michael Bass, may he rest in peace, and Tom is 003. Kathleen only knows the first few by number. Nothing's coming up. She taps away again at the keyboard, shaking her head.

"He's not coming up. He's gone black."

"Are you sure?"

Kathleen looks at Claude and nods her head. "Yes, I'm certain."

"Explain to me again, how this can happen?"

"There are a variety of ways, Claude. He might be traveling underground, through a tunnel as an example, or he might be in the basement of a building. We've tweaked the signal strength as much as we can in these nanos, but you have to understand they're small and the signal fades once a target goes underground by more than eight feet or so, depending on the density of the earth above him or the building material."

"Any other ways?"

"Yes, you could cover yourself with some sort of signal-blocking material."

"What could you use for that purpose?"

"Anything metallic, shiny metallic, lead, aluminum, steel, iron even, depending on the thickness."

"Can the signal be jammed?"

"That's difficult to do. You'd basically have to bathe in radiation or microwaves, and the health effects of that would be adverse. You could also use radio signals to fake a signal, but that's much harder to do with the kinds of signals we use. Additionally, we'd expect to see some signal noise from that type of jamming. We don't see that here, so I think it's being blocked somehow."

Claude sits quietly for a while and then takes the last sip of his champagne.

"Okay," he says. "Everyone in the country, all law enforcement, is looking for Tom, so I'm not worried. I'm sure he'll be picked up sometime today. If not, then we'll clean up this last mess ourselves. I'd like you both back at oh eight hundred tomorrow and we'll see where we are."

"It would be my pleasure to eradicate Tom personally," says James.

Kathleen just nods. She wants this whole thing wrapped up before then. Surely a manhunt for the killer of the president would have Tom snatched up before dawn. She sure hopes so.

5:00 PM

Penn Hills, Pittsburgh

Tom gets up to the crinkle of aluminum foil. In fact, the aluminum kept him in and out of sleep most of the afternoon. It is uncomfortable to wear, and pointy pieces of the helmet kept poking at him uncomfortably. The helmet is almost a full mask, covering everything except his nose and mouth. He pulls it off and puts it on the side table. He managed to make it a quarter of an inch thick. He hopes it had done the trick, or maybe they haven't even started looking for him yet. But that was crazy thinking.

Tom gets out of bed, grabs his IV stand, and walks down the hall looking for a bathroom. He finds it at the end on the left. He places the IV stand on the floor, lifts the toilet seat, and leans against the wall in front of him with his left hand. He unzips his fly and empties his bladder. He puts himself back in place, zips up, and washes his hands. He splashes his face with cold water and takes a long look at himself in the mirror. His eyes look a little sunken but he doesn't look as bad as he'd expected.

He feels pretty good too, hungry, but the fever seems to have subsided and his side is a blunt ache, not the burning hot, tight sensation of infection. He lifts up his shirt and peels back the dressing to take a look.

The inside of the gauze is dotted with just a few flecks of red. His wound is no longer weeping. The stitches are tight and neat. He presses his fingers gingerly around the side of the exit wound. It is achy, but the infection has subsided. Doc is a magician. Tom grabs his IV stand and walks out the bathroom and back down the hall.

"Over here, Tom," says Doc.

Tom looks over to his left and sees Doc in the living room with a bowl of food in his lap. Tom walks in and takes a seat on the other sofa opposite Doc.

"How you feeling, son?" Doc asks.

"Good, thank you. Hungry, but good."

Doc gets up. "I'll get you bowl of lentil soup." And he disappears around a corner and into the kitchen. He's back in no time, carrying one bowl of soup, the steam dancing from its surface like a ghostly belly dancer. On top is placed a big chunk of French bread. A spoon is sticking out of it, its face drowned in the pungent thickness of the lentils. Doc hands it over to Tom.

"Thank you."

"My pleasure. Do you think the tinfoil hat helped?"

"I reckon, otherwise I probably wouldn't be here still. Unless of course they haven't bothered looking for me yet. Though I figure that's slim to none. Probably none."

Tom takes a spoonful of the soup and blows on it before putting it in his mouth. It's still incredibly hot. He tears a chunk off the bread and decides dipping that in the chunky soup is a better idea.

"What's your plan from here, son?"

Tom swallows a mouthful of bread and soup. "I think I'm going to head up to Canada. I know some guys in Toronto. The kind of guys that a guy like me shouldn't know. Guys that probably nobody knows I know. That's the benefit of having worked SOG. The government and even your handlers don't know every detail about what you're up to so long as the job is getting done."

"SOG?"

"Sorry, that's a special branch of the CIA that nobody really talks about. Very secretive, very covert."

Doc nods his head. "Do you have a plan on getting to Toronto?"

Tom smiles at Doc mischievously. "Well, I'm hoping you'll allow me to abuse your kindness and hospitality a little longer."

Tom steadies his gaze on Doc looking for confirmation. Doc nods his head. "Anything you need, son. If I can, I'll help in any way. Maggie says you're vitally important to America's safety and security and to her personally. That's good enough for me."

"Thank you," says Tom, eating mouthfuls of bread and soup in between the conversation. "I need to get to Chinatown, the bad part of Chinatown. I'll also need a lot of money, which I'll repay, if you have it."

"There's not much a Chinatown here in these parts."

"Well, I'll take what I can get. We'll head to the seediest part of town and find a Chinese restaurant, the kind that can help me."

"What's a lot of money to you?"

"Probably twenty to fifty thousand."

"Yup, that is a lot of money."

"Is it something you could access by tomorrow morning, early?"

Doc shakes his head. "Not as cash, but I could come up with it in gold."

"That'll do, if you're willing."

"I'm willing and able." Doc smiles broadly at Tom.

"Thanks, Doc, you have no idea what this means to me. Truly."

"It's not a problem. You said you'd repay it."

"I will, but you're a helluva trusting man."

"At my age, son, it ain't gonna ruin me. If I don't get it back, then I've made a terrible mistake in my judgment of Maggie. And I've never made that kind of character mistake yet."

"Who is Maggie to you, that you'd be willing to go out on a limb for a stranger like me?"

"She's the daughter I never had, a kindred spirit, an old soul like me. We've known each other probably fifteen or so years now. I like to think of myself as her mentor, teacher, and I was her advisor throughout her medical training. She also helped carry me when I couldn't carry on after Lacy, my wife, passed."

"I'm sorry," says Tom.

"Thank you. It's been five years now and life carries on. Anyway, what's your plan with the money."

"I need a change of identity. A passport will cost up to fifty thousand, at least one that's good enough to fool border crossing."

Doc nods and smiles. "You've got yourself in a bit of pickle, haven't you, son?"

Tom tips the bowl of soup to his mouth and empties it. He places it on the coffee table in front of him and nods his head. "Twenty years," he says. "Twenty years I've been serving my country and this is the thanks I get. A bounty on my head. But I aim to make it right. This organization, NANA, needs to be stopped. Assassinating the president is unforgiveable. And men who can do that, there's no telling what they're capable of in the name of righteousness or patriotism. I'm the only one who can bring them down, or at least make them accountable for their actions, if I can live long enough to see it through."

Tom looks down at his feet stretched out before him. His not scared; he's been in life-threatening danger before. But this time, he wonders if the deck is stacked against him, if he can see his way round the obstacles. He sighs.

"I am always cautious of patriotism, Tom," says Doc. "It seems to me a fine line between being proud of one's home and irrational fanaticism. I like it best how Lincoln put it. He said, 'I like to see a man proud of the place in which he lives. I like to see a man live so that his place will be proud of him.'"

Tom looks up at Doc and nods. "I like that. And at the moment it seems that NANA is being steered by nationalistic lunatic at the helm."

11:49 PM

Chinatown (sort of), Pittsburgh

Doc is leading Tom in Doc's Volvo SUV. They drive slowly, a little under the speed limit, and Tom asked they go the quieter, more "scenic" routes to avoid police. They haven't seen any up to this point as they drive into town looking for a place that Tom might like.

Pittsburgh, for a city that grew up chewing on steel, has since put on nice clothes and washed its face. The people represent all the different races and the skyline is modern and clean. Its guts, however, are still dirty, noisy, and rotten, the kind of place Tom spent a lot of time in with the CIA. The violent crime in Pittsburgh is twice the national average. What it lacks in a Chinatown, Tom is confident it made up for in organized crime.

They pass a police van parked on the side of the road, and a couple of officers are talking to a vagrant. Tom is looking for a place to ditch the car. There would be a lot of those sorts of places in the inner city. He just had to find one to his liking.

A couple of blocks up he finds an alley that was all but deserted. Along the right side are cars parked facing away from him. He can see a spot between a couple of them. He flicks his high beams at Doc and pulls into the alley. It is dark; just a little bit of light creeps in like a frightened child, and few squares of light from small windows up the walls in the buildings on each side look cautiously in. Other than that, it is dark as a French Revolution soldier's jacket.

Tom is grateful he stole a small car. He wouldn't have been able to squeeze anything bigger into this small space. He stalls it once he is in there, and thanks to the generosity of Doc, he brought with him a small microfiber facecloth which he uses to take his time to wipe the interior down with. He gets out of the car and closes the door, wiping it with the cloth.

He walks casually back out onto the street and sees Doc pulled over several feet up on his side. He walks up and gets into the car.

"This looks like the kind of place where I could get what I'm looking for," says Tom.

"You want me to come with you?"

"No, I won't be long. I know a Triad-backed restaurant when I see one. That Golden Monkey Palace Peking House is exactly the kind of place I need."

Doc looks down the block halfway and sees the restaurant. Looks like any other Chinese restaurant to him. He nods.

"It shouldn't take me longer than an hour to find a contact and make the deal."

"They make them that quick?"

"No, we'll have to come back in the morning."

Doc nods and hands Tom a small burlap rice bag. Inside is all the gold he owns. It contains two rolls of American Eagles and a sheet of ten Maple Leafs. Tom slides out five Maple Leafs from the sheet.

"I'm not paying them more than this as a down payment," he says. He looks over at Doc. "I really appreciate your kindness. I'll get this back to you." He keeps his eyes steady on Doc. Doc smiles and nods.

"I'm happy to help," he says.

Tom gives the bag back to Doc and opens the door. "I'll be back within the hour. If not, the world's gone to shit and you might as well go home and pretend like you never knew me."

"I'll wait. If you're not back in an hour, I'm coming in after."

"That wouldn't be wise."

"It wouldn't be right to leave a man alone like that."

Tom smiles. "I'll be back before then."

"I'm sure of it."

And Doc watches after him until he enters the door. Doc fiddles with the dial and finds the station he wants. WPGB, smooth jazz all the time.

The restaurant is quiet for this time of night. Only three tables are taken. An attractive waitress walks up to Tom and asks him for how many. Her English is impeccable. Tom answers in Cantonese. She smiles and bats her eyes at him and shows him to a table by the wall.

Tom orders rice noodles with garlic vegetables and a green tea. He watches the waitress head back toward the kitchen. At the angle he's at, he can see into the kitchen, at least a small sliver of it. A well-dressed Chinese man, slim, in his forties with a broken nose and a scar just below his eye, is talking to someone. Probably the cook. This guy looks like the Red Pole. Tom stares at him, seeing if he'll pick up on it. He does. He looks over toward Tom leisurely and locks eyes with him.

His eyes are black like coal. His face is a mask without emotion. He stares at Tom for a while and then looks back to the person he was just talking to. Tom can see he's wearing a gun on his left side. That will most likely make him a lefty.

A few minutes later, the waitress comes back with Tom's tea. It's in a white ceramic pot and she puts down a small white mug next to it that has no handle. She pours him half a cup. Tom thanks her.

Tom keeps watching the kitchen. The Red Pole is looking at someone else and nodding, speaking, but Tom can't hear what they're saying. He gets up and heads toward the washroom, which is down the hall just past the opening of the kitchen he's been looking into. He walks slowly, pretending a limp, and as he passes by the kitchen he glances into it.

Red Pole is talking to another man. He's got salt and pepper hair and stands a few inches taller than Red Pole. His face is sad, like it's been melted and frozen in a frown of wrinkles. He's got a big mole on the upper lip on the left side. The way they're talking, Tom thinks they're equals. They're relaxed, not showing reverence to the other. Tom figures this older man is the Straw Sandal, the guy who can make the introductions.

They ignore him as he passes by and enters the washroom. By the time he gets out and walks back to the table, Straw Sandal is no longer there. Tom notices a door that leads out from the back of the kitchen, maybe into the basement, maybe into back offices. He wants to find out.

In Washington he took out a thousand bucks. He leafs through the money now. Most of the cars he "borrowed" had gas. He counts out $850 and change. He peels a hundred off the stack and rolls it up into his palm. He sits back down at his table.

A few minutes later the waitress comes back with a pile of noodles and vegetables in garlic sauce. Tom smiles at her.

"What's your name?" He's speaking Cantonese.

"Yan T'ien," she says.

"Yan, I want to talk to Straw Sandal, 432."

Tom holds out the hundred dollar bill and puts it in her hand. Yan doesn't say anything for a moment. She looks around guiltily like she's just been found pickpocketing the Benjamin from his pocket.

"Sir, I don't know what you mean."

She's a bad liar, her face is flushed. Tom grabs her wrist, firm but not tight. "Look, Yan, I need the Mountain Master's help. I'm not a cop. I'm just a man who needs a ticket and I've got the money to pay for it."

Tom puts his right hand into his jacket and toys with the gold coins. He's thinking for a moment if he should show her. Would they try and rob him just instead? But he doesn't have the luxury of time. He pulls out three of the gold coins and shows them to her.

"I need a ticket to ride."

He looks her deeply in the eyes, searching for that part of her that will trust him. She looks down pinches her lips and puts her tongue in her cheek for brief moment. Then she looks back up at him.

"Give me a minute."

Her hand squeezes around Benjamin, almost throttling him by the throat. She tucks it into her apron and heads into the kitchen. Tom smells the fragrant garlic and vegetables and decides to tuck in while he waits.

A few minutes later Yan returns with Red Pole. They walk up to his table. Red Pole extends his hand and Tom shakes it. Red Pole's grip is iron and Tom offers the same.

"Sheng Yin," he says.

"Eido Fukushima," says Tom.

Sheng looks at Tom for a moment and then smiles. "If you say so. What can I help you with?"

Sheng sits down opposite Tom and puts his hands on the table, clutching them together. He's leaning in toward Tom.

"I need a ticket, a fresh start." Tom's eating his noodles as he speaks.

"What makes you think we can help with that? Does this restaurant look like a travel agency?" Sheng speaks quietly, thoughtfully. A man used to using words sparsely and carefully as if they were precious jewels.

"Okay," says Tom. "You don't know me. But let me talk to you. I'm going to open my jacket now. I'm going to show you that I am not a cop, I am not wired, and I need to get to Canada right away."

Tom puts down his chopsticks and unzips his jacket. He opens it wide and flaps it around a bit. He puts his hand into his right jacket pocket. "I'm getting the coins."

He puts the coins on the table. Five Maple Leafs. He places them like an exclamation mark in front of Sheng. "This is for the down payment," Tom says. "The rest when I pick up the ticket."

Sheng ignores the gold coins. "You're running from powerful people," he says. "Those risks become our risks."

Tom shrugs, stuffing another mouthful of noodles and vegetables into his face. "If you're good at what you do, nobody can connect the ticket back to you."

"You say you're not a cop, but the TV says otherwise."

Tom looks at Sheng and holds his gaze steady. He picks up the Maple Leafs and places them back in his pocket. "I worked for a secret agency. Organized crime and the likes of you were not our interest. Some people set me up for a fall. If I were here as a sting, we would have had a mole in your organization for months already. That's not our gig."

Tom gets up from the table, puts his hand into his pocket, pulls out his cash and puts a twenty down. "I think I came to the wrong place," he says.

Tom's about to turn around and leave when Sheng waves his hands up to the ceiling and stands up. "You have not come to the wrong place. But what you need will cost you."

"How much?"

"Fifty."

Tom nods.

"Come with me," Sheng beckons.

Tom follows Sheng into the kitchen. Sheng turns around and puts his hand against Tom's chest. "For your safety I will search you."

Tom smiles at him. "Of course."

Tom puts his hands up and Sheng starts patting him down. He comes around his stomach and feels the soft padding of gauze under Tom's shirt. He lifts it up and notices the gauze.

"Do you mind?"

Tom nods.

Sheng peels back the gauze and looks at the gunshot wound. He does the same with the gauze on the other side of Tom's lower back.

"You are lucky."

"I was."

Sheng leads Tom through the backdoor, which opens up into a small waiting room. Straw Sandal is sitting behind a small desk. He looks up at Sheng and Sheng nods.

"He's okay," Sheng says.

"So you need a ticket?" Straw Sandal asks.

Tom nods.

"What country?"

"American."

Straw Sandal looks up at Tom and frowns. "You're a man trying to escape a whole country. That's going to be difficult."

"Not if your ticket's any good."

Straw Sandal chuckles as if Tom were making a joke. "The ticket will get you through, but there's too many eyes on you. That's your problem."

Tom nods his head. "Yes, that is my problem. Can you get the ticket by three."

Straw Sandal looks at Tom like he's just lost his mind. "For a fee."

"How much?"

"Seventy-five."

Tom nods and looks at Sheng. "Yup, I think I've come to the wrong place. All I've got is fifty."

Straw Sandal shakes his head slowly. His frown seems even sadder, as if Tom just told him his kitten has died. Tom turns to leave. As he's about to walk out the door he hears Straw Sandal's voice behind him.

"Sixty is the lowest we can do."

Tom doesn't want to argue nor waste any more time haggling. "Okay," he says. "Do you have clippers, I want to shave my hair off."

Straw Sandal nods his head and gets up behind the desk. He comes round to Tom and holds his hand out to a door on Tom's right. "That is a washroom. Clippers are in the cupboard. Come back out when you're ready."

At twelve thirty in the morning Tom steps out from the restaurant. Doc has been watching all this time, listening to jazz. He doesn't recognize Tom for a split moment with his head shaved, until he's walking toward the car.

"You look a little different. Took me a moment to realize it was you."

"That's the idea," says Tom.

"Went okay?"

Tom nods and smiles. "Good as can be expected, though it's going to cost sixty thousand because of the rush. We can pick it up in a couple of hours."

Doc nods.

"Listen," says Tom, "I need to find a Walmart to buy some cloth so I can make a monk's robe real quick. I think that's the best disguise for me with such short notice."

JASON BLACKER

Doc smiles. "A man after my own heart. I can do better than that. I can give you my uttarasanga and antaravasaka. When my wife died I took a pilgrimage to a Buddhist monastery for six months."

Tom grins. "Wow, kismet has been kind to me ever since I met you."

Doc starts up the car and they drive back to Penn Hills to tailor the robe for Tom's height.

6:17 AM

Outside Buffalo, New York

Buffalo is one of those small towns you see all over the world. The kind with open arms and warm hugs. The kind of town slick with service and feel-good attitude. These are the tourist towns. They're bathing in money from folks coming across with bucket lists in one hand and fat wallets in the other. So long as you've got money and a camera around your neck, you're best friends. Life takes a turn for the worse; you're down on your luck. Well, good luck partner; keeping hiking down the road.

If you really want to take a look at the ugly underneath the fake smiles, you only have to wait a while until a real recession hits. The smiles become hungry, and if you've got any whiff of money you'll be chewed up and spat out faster than you can say "Where's the tourist information center?"

Tom hasn't been to Buffalo before. He hasn't ever seen the Niagara Falls. This would be a treat if he were a tourist. But he isn't a tourist. He is a man on the lam, and the wolves are nipping at his heels.

He left everything in sleepy Penn Hills with Doc. His 1911 was a gift for Doc as were the two extra mags. His wallet and real ID were left behind too. The ID was left burned to ashes. All Tom has is a small satchel that blends well with his orange uttarasanga. Under the uttarasanga he wears a sarong called an antaravasaka, which covers his waist down to his knees. It is natural in color, and under that he wears boxer briefs. Tom isn't sure if those are regulation monk wear, but they sure make him feel less naked.

And speaking of naked, that's exactly how he feels. Even though the robe covers him from neck to ankles—except for a smooth right shoulder, naked like a peeking sun at dawn, and his right arm, he was covered thoroughly—still, he feels naked, even under the robe's comforting heavy weight.

But he does feel peaceful and serene, almost spiritual. The feeling crept over him shortly after he put on the robe and looked in the mirror at Doc's house. He had heard it said that the clothes make the man, but Tom always thought it was the uniform that made the soldier. He remembered how proud and confident he felt whenever he put on his service dress for navy functions. The clothes you wear lend an air of psychological weight to your overall psyche.

Sitting in the passenger seat watching Doc drive through Buffalo, Tom feels he has gained several layers of enlightenment, just sitting in his orange robe. The true test will come, however, when he goes to buy his ticket, and more so when they are at the Canadian border.

The original plan was to have Doc drop him off at the Pittsburgh greyhound station, but the timing didn't work well for that stop. The earliest he would've gotten into Toronto would be 5:00 PM. Time is not his ally on this occasion. He needs to get across the border as quick as possible before they start doubling up the security at every border crossing. All going well, he should be through customs a little after eight. If he makes it through at all.

Tom looks through his satchel again. It is small, smaller than a woman's handbag, and mostly empty. Inside is his new passport. He takes it out and looks at it again. The quality is excellent, and so it should be for sixty grand. He can't tell the difference between it and a real one. Straw Sandal assured him it will get him through the border. When Tom asked him if there was a money-back guarantee behind that assurance, the old Chinese man laughed good-naturedly. Still, if this passport won't get him through, Tom isn't sure which one will.

He puts the passport back into the satchel and pulls out a small multi-colored cotton-knit coin purse. It is a little larger than a credit card but it doesn't contain any credit or debit cards inside. Tom left those with Doc, with the passwords. Not that it'd help; his accounts have probably been frozen or will be anytime now. Not that it is a big loss. Tom doesn't keep most of his money in the bank. He keeps it in chunks all over the world in lockers in bus stations, airports, and other places.

He zips open the purse and takes a look inside. There are four Benjamins, eight Grants, two Jacksons, and a Hamilton all sleeping together peacefully, their political differences put to bed. Along with that he has some coins. At the bottom of the purse he tears away a side of the purse from its Velcro enclosure. Inside are five Maple Leafs. These were a gift from Doc.

Straw Sandal took the five Maple Leafs as a deposit, and Tom gave up thirty-five American Eagles in exchange for the passport. Doc insisted Tom take the rest of the gold coins, but Tom couldn't do that in good faith. He suggested, seeing as he was going to Canada, he'd take the five remaining Maple Leafs and, seeing how Doc was staying in the US, he should keep the five remaining Eagles. Seemed only fair. Doc went for it, but not without protesting a bit first.

Doc pulls up on Ellicott Street. The bus station is just across from them. Doc turns the radio off and turns to Tom. "How you feeling, son?"

Tom puts the purse back in the satchel and closes the satchel up. "Honestly?"

Doc nods and smiles kindly.

"Scared as shit. If I don't get through this, I'm as good as dead. If I do get through this, I might die in my sleep tonight, or tomorrow, or however long I can hold out."

Doc's nodding his head. "I understand," he says. "Do you want me to wait here for a bit?"

"No. Here on out I'm on my own. But listen, Doc. I really appreciate everything you've done for me these last couple of days. Really."

Doc puts a big ham-sized hand on Tom's covered shoulder. "I'd do the same for my friends," he says, grinning like a Cheshire cat.

Tom laughs out loud. He's glad Doc broke the ice. It feels better to laugh off some of the nervousness.

"Be in touch, Tom."

Tom nods, putting his right hand by the door lever. "I will," he says. "Speaking of keeping in touch, please don't reach out to Margaret for another twenty-four hours at least. And when you do, don't give away much. They'll be tapping all her phones, probably the email accounts that they know about."

"I will."

Tom opens the door and he's about to get out of the car. Doc squeezes his shoulder again. Tom turns and looks at him.

"Be careful, son," Doc says. "I want to hear you made it safe when you can send word."

"I will."

"For Maggie too. She likes you, you know?"

"I know."

"I mean, she really likes you."

Doc holds Tom's gaze steady for a moment. Tom smiles at him. "I know."

Then he's out the car and Doc's watching him walk into the bus station. The last image he sees is of a devout Buddhist monk in flowing orange robes. Tom wears it well. Doc's not as fearful for him as he might otherwise be.

6:36 AM

Buffalo, New York

There aren't many people in the bus station. Maybe it's too early for tourists to be up and about. There are just two other people in the line for the ticket window. In front of Tom is an old man carrying an old-fashioned suitcase. Looks like the best days are behind him. The best thing about him is his hair, which is wispy, white, and covering his scalp like threadbare muslin.

Even standing a couple of feet from the old man, Tom can smell the reek of tobacco on him. The old man glances sideways and Tom can see a big red nose stuck on his face like squashed putty. It's purple, swollen, pockmarked, and spidered. Most likely been dipped into way too much liquor in its day.

The first person in the line is just finishing up grabbing his ticket and paying for it. Looks like a college kid. He's got his backpack on him. He's wearing blue jeans and a lumberjack's jacket. His hair is bird's nest of blonds and browns. The kid's young and carefree, looks like he's mother's just finished bathing him. He pulls out crinkled cash, lint, and a small rectangle of chewing gum out of his pocket to pay.

He finishes up pretty quickly and the old man steps forward. His shoulders stoop like he's carrying all the world's burdens. His red soft plastic suitcase doesn't look like it's too heavy. It doesn't make his shoulders stoop anymore.

Tom looks around. He feels pious and peaceful, wrapped up like a bug in a rug. A few folk take a look at him but then pass their gaze onto other more interesting things. He likes that. Even though he stands out like a sore thumb, he's not that noticeable. Folks aren't paying him a lot of attention. Buddhist monks are, after all, non-threatening.

Tom watches the old man fumble through a wallet that looks as old as he does. The edges of the leather are worn bare. He pulls out his money. Maybe it's a hundred bucks in there, and he puts the wallet down on the counter. The wallet lies empty, its mouth a gaping hole like a fish out of water. The old man counts out his money carefully, hoping he'll find more than he knows he has.

He puts down three Jacksons and they're facing him, their frowning eyes asking questions he doesn't know the answer to. The old man gets his change and ticket, while Tom takes out the coin purse from his satchel. The old man carefully puts the change back in his wallet, the bills all neat and ironed out straight in order of face value. He holds onto the ticket and turns around while he tries to put his wallet back into his bag. He stumbles, his wallet dropping like a sandwich, and he bumps into Tom.

"Sorry," he says.

"Namaste," Tom replies.

Tom swims through a heady vapor of liquor. The old man smells like he just came out of a brewery. Tom bends down and picks up the old man's wallet and hands it back to him. The old man's face crinkles into a smile and it makes him look a lot better.

"Thank you," he says shyly. He picks up his suitcase and hurries off as fast as a tortoise.

"Can I help you?"

Tom looks up and smiles at the ticket woman. She looks him up and down and for some reason she smiles back, her hard face chipped into something softer.

"One ticket to Toronto please."

Tom smiles again. The woman smiles.

"Forty-five dollars and sixty-eight cents."

Tom digs into his coin purse and pulls out the two Jacksons and the Hamilton. He offers them to her. She takes them.

"You need a passport to cross into Canada. Can I see your passport please?"

Tom hands her his passport. She looks at it and flips to the photograph. She looks at that and then at him.

"Good," she says. "You'll need to hold onto that for crossing the border."

She hands Tom his passport and then his ticket and change.

Tom bows his head and brings his hands up to his chest as if in prayer. "Thank you."

"You're welcome," she says. "The bus leaves at seven. Wait at exit number three." She points to a group of people standing around exit three. Tom looks at them and then back at her. He nods again, puts his money away, and takes his ticket.

"This is easier than it seems," he thinks to himself.

Tom heads over to the group of travelers and waits. He doesn't have to wait long. Minutes later, they start boarding the bus. Tom is offered a place in the line ahead of a couple of young men. He likes the preferential treatment men of the cloth seem get. He enters the bus and sees the young backpacker already seated in the middle. Tom heads toward the back of the bus. He's hoping it'll be safer and more discreet, so long as Canadian border agents don't decide to walk all the way down to the end and take a special interest in him. He's hoping they're not on the look out for a Tomo Daisen.

At the back of the bus is a copy of the Buffalo News. The front page has a picture of Tom. He looks at it. It's one of his earlier Navy pictures in service dress. It's not the best picture of anyone if you're hoping the general public will take notice. That gives him some relief.

Tom scans the rest of the article. They've decided that he's heading to New York City where he has family. At least, that's what the police are telling the papers. That's good for him. The FBI is leading the investigation and urging the public to call the hotline if they see anyone they suspect as Tomo Daisen. The FBI is urging the public not to take matters into their own hands, and they've notified the New York Police Department and all other agencies in New York to be on the lookout.

The bus heads out of the station. It's about one-third full. Tom figures there are about two dozen or so souls traveling with him. Tom looks out the window and sees Doc's car is still parked where he left it. Doc's waving through the window. Tom gives him a reverent bow with his hands together. He's going to stay in character until he's safely in Toronto, where it'll be time for another change.

At around seven fifteen in the morning the bus comes to a stop behind another charter bus in the bus lane on Peace Bridge Plaza. It seems to take forever for them to move. It is probably only around five minutes and then Tom's bus lurches forward and Tom's stomach lurches with it into his throat. The bus driver gets up and faces them.

"I'm going to come around and get your passports," he says. "Please have them ready."

Everyone starts rifling through their bags as the driver walks slowly up the aisle. Tom's is the last passport he picks up. The bus driver returns to his seat and then opens up the door and a Canada border agent boards the bus. The driver and the agent banter for a few moments, obviously on friendly terms.

Tom is trying to hear what is being said without making it obvious. Now he wishes he were closer. He thinks he sees the agent mouth the words "Asian-American on board," and the bus driver sort of points toward the back of the bus and mouths what looks to Tom like "Buddhist monk." The agent nods and starts looking through the passports. Tom figures he came to his last, as he seems to look at it for a long time. Then the agent's radio goes off. It is loud.

"Asian suspect being uncooperative. Request assistance."

The voice is heavy with exertion. The agent nods at the bus driver and says something that likely means we can go. He hands the last passport back to the bus driver and gets off the bus in a hurry.

"Thank God for small mercies," thinks Tom.

The bus driver gets up and hands back the passports, looking at the photographs and then offering them back to the passenger. Again he comes to Tom last. By this stage Tom's heart is beating like a drum in his chest. He just wants to get the hell across the border.

The bus driver seems to take his sweet time getting back into his seat and buckling up. Looks to Tom like the guy is either trying to stretch out Tom's suffering or he is stuck in molasses. The bus starts forward and then stops abruptly again. Tom cranes to see what is going on, his heart banging around like a frightened bird in his cage of ribs.

A border agent runs across the front of the bus. The bus starts off again and Tom breathes a sight of relief. He looks out to his left and sees a few border agents wrestling with a group of young Asian men. This is the first time in his life Tom is grateful for racial profiling. Those young men likely saved the day for him.

The bus takes a few minutes to get onto the Peace Bridge, and Tom looks out the right window. Cheers erupt from some of the passengers as the bus driver welcomes them into Canada. Tom feels like a weight has lifted off his shoulders. He is one step closer to figuring out how to bring NANA down. He closes his eyes and tries to meditate without falling asleep. He is tired. Drained and hungry.

7:57 AM

Fleming, Greene and Le Carré, LLC, Washington D.C.

Claude stands and looks out the window. He can see most of the parking lot attached to this professional building. It is a square grey slab of tarmac. Claude has his arms crossed and he's resting his chin on his left thumb and index finger. He's watching Margaret get out of her car. She's wearing blue slacks and a white blouse under a blue blazer.

It seems she's had a thing for Tom for some time. You can see it in the way she talks to him when she's setting him up for dreamscape erasure. You can see it in the lingering touches. Just a little longer than they need to be.

Claude's worried about it. It's the official policy of NANA not to allow for the mixing of company ink. Folks will get fired for it. Hasn't happened yet, but it might come soon. Claude watches Margaret close her door and open the driver side passenger door. She leans over, and Claude admires her figure. He can see how a man could fall for her. If that man wasn't in control of himself.

Love is a slippery eel and he doesn't it like it. It brings unknowns into the equation. That's a problem. Human personalities being as unreliable in the long run as they are, adding love is like setting a match to a powder keg. It's going to go off at some point.

Margaret is closing the passenger door having got out her laptop and bag. She starts walking toward the main entrance of the office building Claude is in. Claude watches her until she disappears from sight. He's concerned she's become a lit powder keg. Claude has his misgivings about Margaret's loyalty to NANA. He thinks she's started to lean on Tom's side.

Sometimes Claude wishes everything was under his control. It would be so much easier that way. As it is, he's made a request for her telephone records, though they being personal phones his people use, it was rejected. That pissed him off. It meant he had to make a detour this morning to a judge and bring in a favor. The subpoena for Margaret's phone records were just sent off not half an hour before.

By this evening he should have the information he requires. While he was at it, he subpoenaed the phone records of James, Kathleen, and Anthony, just to put his mind at ease. He's not worried about James and Anthony. They're career men who take orders well without questioning them. Kathleen is a civilian who might be uncomfortable with what part she's played. He wants to keep tabs on her. She's as guilty as the rest of them, and that ought to keep her on a short leash.

Claude walks across his room toward the painting by Copley and admires the subtlety of it. He looks closely at the naked Brook Watson in the green water. Watson has lost his right leg below the knee. Likely NANA will have to cut away some of the dead flesh too. Time will tell, but that's a sacrifice Claude is willing to make if need be.

His phone rings and he goes over to it and picks it up.

"Dr. Margaret Rakes is here to see you, sir. Shall I send her into the boardroom with the others?" asks the receptionist.

"No, send her in to my office."

Claude puts down the phone and walks around to his side of the desk where he sits down. A moment later there's a knock on his door.

"Come in."

Jeannine Alonzo, NANA's receptionist, opens the door and lets Margaret in behind her. She closes the door behind her as she leaves. Claude looks at Margaret for a moment. Her hands are clasped in front of her, clutching her purse. Her laptop is slung over her right shoulder. She glances furtively at him. Claude can tell she's nervous.

"Please come and sit down for a moment."

Margaret sits down, putting her purse on her lap and her hands over the top of it like a shroud. Her laptop still hangs from her right shoulder. "It must be heavy," thinks Claude. He smiles at her. A wolf in sheep's clothing who's just swallowed the shepherd.

"You know why you're here?"

She nods. "To find Tom."

"That's part of the reason. The other part is to evaluate your commitment to me, to NANA."

Margaret swallows uncomfortably. She's feeling hot all of a sudden. "I am committed to NANA, sir."

"I hope so, Margaret. For your sake, I really hope so."

"I'm here to help you find Tom."

"Where else could you be?"

She thinks about a response for a moment but decides against any. She understands the veiled threat underneath those words.

"I must be honest," continues Claude, "about your performance the other night. If I were paranoid I might have suspected you were helping Tom."

He keeps his gaze steady on her. She looks down at his desk. It's an old wooden desk. She can see the marks of time in it. She wishes time would just hurry up and get all this over with. She's not sorry she helped Tom, but she also knows the cost to her might very well be her life. She looks back up at him and holds his gaze.

"I was tired and I just got flustered, that's all. Tom came out of Theta so suddenly asking for EOL confirmation, I wasn't ready for it."

It sounded like a legitimate reason to her ears. Claude smiles.

"Perhaps," he says. "I'd like your phone."

"Why?"

"Just to be certain you haven't been corresponding with the enemy."

She doesn't want to give it to him, but she doesn't have a choice. Not giving it over will be a sure sign of guilt. "Besides," she thinks, "he's probably subpoenaed the records anyway." She's grateful she erased all history of their text messages, but perhaps she should have lost her phone like Tom suggested. Though that wouldn't look good anyway.

Margaret reaches into her purse and pulls out her phone and hands it over to Claude. He opens it up and goes to unlock it.

"What's the password?"

"Six–three–seven–four."

He searches through all her history, both calls and texts and emails but he doesn't find anything related to Tom. He smiles at her.

"This is good news," he says, "so long as the records back this up, everything will be good for you. If it doesn't, well then, I needn't remind you of the nanos coursing through your body as we speak."

Margaret wavers. She glances down at her purse, and if you're watching carefully you'll see the sides of her mouth twitch. She wonders if they'd really kill her over such a small indiscretion. Maybe they—whoever the hell "they" are— wouldn't, but she wouldn't put it past Claude.

"Come, let's join the others," he says, "and figure out where the hell Tom is."

About Jason Blacker

Jason Blacker was born in Cape Town but spent most of his first 18 years in Johannesburg. When not grinding his fingers down to stubs at the keyboard he enjoys drinking tea, calisthenics and running. Currently he lives in Canada.

Under his own name he writes hard boiled as well as cozy mysteries, action adventure, thrillers, literary fiction and anything else that tickles his muse. Jason Blacker also writes poetry and daily haikus at his haiku blog.

You can find his haikus and other poetry at his website **www.haiqueue.com**.

To stay up to date and learn about new releases be sure to visit **www.jasonblacker.com** where you can find more information about his writing and upcoming projects.

If you enjoy space opera in the tradition of Star Trek then take a look at Jason Blacker's pen name "Sylynt Storme". It is under the name **Sylynt Storme** where you can find both sci-fi and vampire fiction written by Jason Blacker.

"Star Sails" is the space opera series and **"The Misgivings of the Vampire Lucius Lafayette"** is his vampire series.